MY SWEET VALENTINE

DEBBIE CHASE

This is a work of fiction. Names, characters, places, and incidents are products of the author's imagination or are used fictitiously and are not to be construed as real. Any resemblance to actual events, locations, organizations, or persons, living or dead, is entirely coincidental.

World Castle Publishing, LLC
Pensacola, Florida

Paperback ISBN: 9798891262867
eBook ISBN: 9798891262874
First Edition World Castle Publishing, LLC, October 28, 2024
http://www.worldcastlepublishing.com

Licensing Notes

Cover: Cover Designs by Karen
Cover-designs-by-karen.com
Editor: Karen Fuller

For Mum and Dad on their 66th Wedding Anniversary
4 October 1958 to 4 October 2024
Congratulations
I am So Proud of You

CHAPTER ONE

Present Day

I lived on a boat, well I suppose I should have called it a barge or maybe a narrowboat, being that they're slightly different from just the usual boat, on the canal in a small market town called Hebden Bridge, in West Yorkshire. It had been voted as "the fourth funkiest town in the world," which was so true as it's packed with wonderful little shops bursting at the seams with quirky jewelry and vintage, and there were loads of really cool pubs and restaurants and music venues.

It was surrounded by scenic walks; you could stroll along the river as it curled beside grassy banks or ramble through Hardcastle Crags. There was a brilliant little village nearby called Heptonstall boasting two pubs and a beautiful church where the poet, Sylvia Plath, was buried, and there was also Lumb Bank, a fine house where Ted Hughes had lived, a great poet but a lousy husband to Sylvia, apparently.

Under normal circumstances, I would have been impressed by this place no end, but in my present state of mind? Um, perhaps not! I dwelt on my state of mind often, sometimes early in the morning, sipping a hot strong coffee, gazing from my boat's little porthole window at the still, brown waters of the canal, watching the September mist hanging over it like a hazy ceiling, or watching the swans swim oh so regally, orange legs kicking, as ducks quack and naughty geese honk morning noon and night. I dwelt on my state of mind at night as well, whilst sipping red wine from a great balloon of glass as the half-light of the day lit up the inky sky twinkling with stars and the great globe of the moon as it shone like a lantern in the blackness.

Now, just wait a minute. I was getting carried away there, and before I went on with my story, I really ought to have introduced myself. I mean, I could have been anybody, couldn't I? You need to know who I was. In fact, you deserve to know who I was. So here goes. My name was Jenny, or Jennifer, as my mum used to call me when I was a naughty girl many moons ago, Jenny Clarke, and up until approximately a year ago, I was living with Dave, my boyfriend of two years. Dave Ledgard, IT Extraordinaire, in a three-bedroom semi in Todmorden, a place known as Tod to the locals.

I'd thought we were okay, happy even until

Dave told me he was applying for a new job. I was interested and excited, it being very well paid, creating flashing pound signs in my mind's eye, as didn't we always need the extra money? My mind roamed over all the things we could do with it, firstly a holiday, a hot sultry holiday, and then we could do repairs to the house, a new bathroom suite would be nice, a power shower, a tarmacked drive instead of the gravelly mess we had at the moment until that is, he told me the job was in America. New York, to be precise.

I remember I'd laughed and said, "Don't be daft, Dave, you can't go to America."

"No," he replied, "But *we* can!" He gave me a conspiratorial side-eyed wink.

I'd looked at him, surprised. I'd even giggled a bit, "I can't go to America, Dave. In case you've forgotten, I happen to have a very pregnant daughter right here in Tod. Do you really think I'd want to go all that way and miss out on my first grandchild? Actually, this could be my only grandchild."

"Nah, she'll have more surely. You'll have loads of grandchildren all clamoring for your attention. You wait and see." He gave a decided "I've made my mind up" nod of the head.

"Dave," I replied patiently, "Emma's my only child, so exactly how many children do you think she's going to have? And you saying I might have loads of grandchildren has made it worse, made it more impossible to leave here. Don't you see?"

He gave a non-committal shrug, "Well, I'm still going to have a stab at this, Jen. Someday, I'll be too old, past it, you know what I mean."

"We're not even fifty yet," I replied.

"Time flies," he said with a grin, "Time flies, Jen, and before you know it, pouff, you're gone."

And then he did something unexpected, something out of character. He came close and pulled me into his arms, kissed my cheek, his lips soft and moist. I remembered the good, solid warmth of his body pressed against mine, and suddenly, my heart sank, and I came back to the present, thoughts running through my head. "Had I made a mistake?" "What had I done, letting him go like that, all by himself."

Gazing around, my heart sank even further as I saw the inside of the boat as if for the very first time, the tiny kitchen cum sitting area, the curtained-off bedroom, the small screened TV, my little pink CD player, my phone blank faced at my side. Poor and sparse as I thought back to the large open rooms of the semi I'd lived in before.

I felt as cold and as lonely as when Frank, my husband of twenty-five years, had died. Emma's doting Dad. Without realizing it, my life with Dave had brought me back to life. Oh God, what had I done?

My heart raced, and I put my hand over my mouth, trying to take long, even breaths to calm myself. A voice brought me out of my reverie, and glancing up, I gazed straight into a pair of mossy green eyes and a mouth soft and pink that moved beautifully as he said, "Hi, is this your cat?"

"My cat? Why, yes." I held out my arms to take her, my erratically beating heart temporarily forgotten, "Why? What happened?"

"Um, just had a feeling she was going to jump into the water, and well, I picked her up before she had a chance."

I laughed, "Yeah, she does that sometimes, but don't worry, she's a good swimmer." And then to the cat, "Hey, Sydney, are you okay, girl?" She snuggled into my arms, simultaneously meowing and purring into my neck.

He laughed, creating a myriad of wrinkles around his eyes and dimples, too, one on either side of his mouth, "Sydney? You mean after the girl in "Scream? The film?"

"Well, yeah, but not only that, I just really like the name, you know, especially for a girl..."

He nodded seriously, "Yeah, I like it, too."

"What's your dog called?" I asked, noticing a great white fluffy ball sitting patiently at his side.

"Ah yes, please meet Ziggy Stardust in all his

glory." He gave a mock theatrical bow, pointing his fingers at the dog who gave me what could only be called a smile, all his little white teeth showing. I was charmed but managed to tear my eyes away to say, "David Bowie, eh?"

"Oh yes, massive fan."

"Me too. I saw him only once in concert, in the nineties. He was great, but I really wished I'd seen him earlier, in the seventies maybe, when he was actually Ziggy … before he killed him off."

"Yeah, well, I did. Hey, don't get jealous, will you?"

We grinned at each other, our eyes locking, his very green and mine, a strange color, green flecked with yellowish bits, hazel, I think it's called. My heart thumped so hard, right up into my ears, that surely, he could hear it? I felt sort of weak and watery, my knees bendy as pipe cleaners. What was wrong with me? Suddenly, my phone rang shrilly from my pocket, causing Sydney to tense up and jump, landing with a thump on the deck and then shooting off inside to hide under the bed, no doubt.

"Oh well," I tapped my pocket, "I'd better go. Nice to talk to you, um?"

He nodded and smiled again, those very attractive wrinkles appearing again around his eyes and the dimples on either side of his mouth, "Andy

Valentine, pleased to meet you, and?" He put his head to one side, a questioning look on his face.

"Really? Andy Valentine?"

Frowning, he said, "Yeah … how about you?"

My phone carried on ringing and ringing, a burring sound as it pulsated against my thigh. Retrieving it from my pocket, I glanced at the screen, the name "Dave" clearly visible. My heart thumped, *"Why was he ringing me? Couldn't he take to his new life? Was he coming back?"*

"I'm Jenny Clarke. Look, I'm sorry, but I really have to take this call."

"Sure," he grinned, "See you around, um, hopefully."

I nodded and said, "Yeah," as I rushed inside, putting my phone to my ear.

"Hello?"

"Wow, you took a long time. I thought you'd fallen in the water. Jenny, I can't believe you're living on a boat…"

"Dave? Are you okay? I mean, phoning all the way from America! It must be an emergency." He laughed as I said, "We've been through this before. I like living here on the boat." Peering through the window, I could just about make out the man called Andy Valentine slowly walking away, his stride long and loose, the smiling dog Ziggy padding at his side.

"Well, is there an emergency?" I giggled, "This call is so unexpected."

"Nothing wrong, no emergency, Jenny, actually everything is very right. I'm sitting here in my office, looking from the window, a fabulous view of Manhattan spread out all around me. I can even see Central Park from here like a little green oasis in its concrete world. Now, wouldn't you like to see that sort of view from your window, Jen? Inspiration for your writing? Or are you happy with the murky brown waters of the canal at Hebden Bridge? Come on now, be truthful."

I hesitated for a moment, gazing around again at the cluttered interior of the boat, the view of rippling canal water from the tiny porthole, the sound all-around of quacking ducks and irate geese, the graceful paddling of swans, the leaves on the trees whispering as they shivered in the breeze. I squeezed through the boat's tiny doorway onto the deck and sat down on my one and only rickety deck chair, the sun warm on my shoulders.

"Jenny?"

"Yeah, sorry, I was trying to think of a good answer."

"How about the truth?"

"I like it here, Dave. Yeah, okay, I'm living on a boat at the moment, but, well," I shrugged, "I like it here. That's about it, really."

He sighed heavily as, in the distance, I heard the manic sound of a telephone ringing and ringing, "You know, Jen, I don't know if I believe you, but I gotta go. My phone's ringing. I'll be in touch, yeah?"

"Okay, Dave, I…" There was a click as the phone disconnected, so I clicked off too and carefully put my mobile back in my pocket, and stayed sitting there, my face turned to the sun. The warmth burning into my skin was luxurious, as was the bright orange glow that blossomed at the back of my eyes. I was just about to tell Dave I missed him, so, really, it was just as well, he'd rung off. I didn't want him to sense a weakness in me and think I couldn't cope alone, that I regretted letting him go. Even though I did, sometimes.

My thoughts turned back to the man, Andy Valentine, and a hot tremor tore through my body as the thought, "He was flirting with me," rushed through my mind. A sense of surprise overwhelmed me at the thought that a good-looking man would even bother with me at the moment. I was well aware of the shapeless sack I'd become since Dave had gone.

I saw myself in my mind's eye, the overgrown bush of hair, lacking any discernible style, the ends dry and in dire need of a cut, the same old clothes day in and day out, creased denim shorts and a vest top for the heat, jeans, and a tee-shirt, a too big hoodie pulled over the top when it grew cold. Even my shoes were a mess, shabby trainers complete with frayed laces that slopped around on my feet like boats.

And yet…I opened my eyes and gazed up at the great expanse of the sky, scattered with fluffy clouds that looked like comfortable fat cushions spread across a blue settee. Andy Valentine had flirted with me. Something I hadn't even thought about happening after all the years, first with Frank and then Dave. A slow, satisfied smile stole across my face as I closed my eyes and let go, dozing into the heat.

***

I was a writer of romance novels. My pen name Claudia Raines (which, incidentally, my daughter, Emma, wasn't a big fan of), *"Sounds too much like that old actor, Claude Raines, Mum."* She had been right. It did, but hey, what was wrong with that? He had been a great actor, so I wasn't going to change it. It was too late now. I had been published with that name (after many years and a ton of hard work), so I thought it was lucky, far luckier than plain old Jenny Clarke, that was for sure, or even when I'd used my married name of Smith. Yes, Smith. Could you understand then, why I had a pen name, dear reader? The only thing was, romance writing was one of the worst professions to be in when you were down and depressed, especially if you had the blues because of your relationship, because of your other half, or because of a man.

Your thoughts dried up, and romance went out of the window, so how could you write about it? How could you bear to write about happy couples, putting down in words that first all-important meeting, like a display of beautiful fizzing fireworks, the catastrophe halfway through the story that almost split them up, and the pure unadulterated making up at the end, bringing them back together again? So, I'm pretty much stuck at the moment, my living having dried up, a bank balance, once as healthy as a marathon runner, now at a very low ebb, and yet, my savings were untouched so far, which is how I want them to stay.

I needed to get back into it, and get focussed. After all, I had a granddaughter now, baby Milly, who I wanted to spoil, who I wanted to buy things for, lots of toys, cute dresses, and tiny shoes, ready and waiting for her very first steps. Emma was visiting with Milly that afternoon, but first of all, in my quest to get my thoughts running again, I had taken myself away from the boat and come to a nearby café, slap bang in the center of Hebden Bridge, an old cottage facing onto the canal, my boat bobbing on the water only a stone's throw away.

"Classy Coffee" was a vibrant place with a friendly feel where I could sit, my laptop wide open in front of me, a cup of fragrant coffee at my side,

hey, maybe even a pastry. I looked around, my gaze taking in the bumpy white-washed walls, at black and white pictures of a very old Hebden Bridge, as well as local quirky art, including drawings, paintings, and sculptures amassed on the deep window sills. I took in the beamed ceiling and the stone-flagged floor where round wooden tables stood covered with red and white checked cloths, an empty wine bottle on each, candles dribbling wax stuck into each one.

The waitresses, wearing tight black skirts, half buttoned shirts, covered by long black aprons, their skin, particularly arms, necks, and legs, decorated with colorful tattoos, walked quickly from table to table, holding trays high above their heads, theatrically depositing their contents onto each table, that were full of chattering people, eager for food and drink, for talk and gossip. The coffee machine whooshed steam, and piped music flowed delicately from hidden speakers.

I took a sip of hot, strong coffee, followed by a bite of the soft pastry, and stared at the screen of my laptop, the title of the novel I was trying to write in bold black letters right in front of my eyes, *"Hidden Desires,"* followed by the words, *"Jeanette's thoughts turned to last night, to Henry. She recalled his eyes, dark as sloes as they gazed into hers, the feeling of skin on skin, his kisses that rained passionately onto her lips…"*

"Oh, what tosh," I thought, as once again,

I raised my coffee cup to my lips and took a long swallow, feeling its energy rushing through my veins, giving me a much-needed boost. With a quick press of the delete button, I erased the words about Jeanette and Henry (Henry indeed, maybe Harry would be better? Or Josh, yes, with a sudden blinding knowledge, I knew he had to be called Josh), leaving just the title *"Hidden Desires,"* which gazed reproachfully at me from the screen, wanting I knew more words. "Explain yourself," I could almost hear it say, "Come on, Jen, explain yourself, reveal your hidden desires. Come on, write, get writing. Come on, surprise yourself, girl."

"Oh dear," I thought, "Where was my usual flair for words? This was the worst writer's block I'd ever had!" I carried on berating myself, making God only knows what strange faces as I mumbled, when I sensed a presence at my side, a male presence, carrying a tray containing something that smelled delicious, hot and steaming on a plate, a silver teapot, with a matching tiny jug and a cup and saucer.

"Well, hi," I said coming face to face with the man, Andy Valentine, his eyes green as grass, locking with mine.

"Would you mind if I shared your table?" he asked, shrugging and gazing self-consciously around, "Everywhere else is full."

"Of course," I said, ducking my head to hide a

face that had begun to burn, my cheeks aflame, as my heart started to beat hard and fast at the thought of the last time I'd spoken with this man. What a weird effect he seemed to have on me. Hastily, I moved my laptop to one side and pulled my mug towards me, as well as my plate with its half-eaten pastry. He smiled at me as he sat down, his dimples appearing as if by magic, his green eyes glittering in a band of sunlight that fell through the large plate glass window onto the table.

Carefully he put his tray down, saying, "Well, it's really good to see you again," Seeming flustered, he blushed a little as he rambled on, "I was hoping to see you again and, oh, um, well, thanks for letting me share." Smiling a little, he sat down and, slowly, shyly even, began to eat, nodding at the laptop, "Are you working? Sorry if I've interrupted you."

I sighed, "I'm trying to work, but unfortunately, I'm not getting very far. A bit of writer's block, I think." Putting my arms above my head, I stretched, rolling my neck a few times to relieve the stiffness.

"Oh," he put down his knife and fork and poured tea from the silver pot into his cup, adding milk and then maybe a grain or two of sugar, "You're a writer? Wow."

"Careful with the sugar, eh?" And then, "Yes, romance novels and the romance just isn't coming today."

He laughed, "Yeah, I don't like too much sugar. A grain or two is far too much, really." He patted his slim stomach as our gaze met again whilst he sliced a piece of quiche and put it into his mouth, chewing and swallowing before saying, "Hmm, maybe you get your romance at home?" He gave me a sideways glance.

"Oh no," I told him, "There's none of that at home. I mean," I stammered, "I live alone." Once again, I felt a hot blush suffuse my face.

He nodded as he took another sip, "Oh, I see. It's up to the imagination, then?"

I smiled and laughed, "Yes, and I usually have quite a good one, but ..."

"Not today?"

"No, not today."

The people at the next table began to leave, their chairs scraping on the flagged floor, their voices loud with exclamations of thanks as they made their way out of the café, and the door pinged closed behind them. One of the waitresses swept in like a seagull, clearing the table of all its debris in the blink of an eye.

I gazed at him, Andy Valentine, secretly from the corner of my eye. He wore jeans with a black leather belt and a blue shirt tucked in, the top buttons of which were undone, showing a good expanse of curly chest hair. His beard was black and stubbly, sprinkled finely over his cheeks and chin, and his lips looked soft and pink, his tongue flicking in and out as he ate and drank. My heart thumped like somebody banging a drum, Roger Taylor, I hoped in his days as a drummer with Queen.

Having finished his meal, he picked up his cup and sipped his tea before asking casually, "So you're not married then?"

"I was," I told him, "But my husband died…"

"Oh, I'm sorry…"

For something to do, I picked up the half-eaten pastry and nibbled at it nervously, "Oh, he's been gone for more than ten years now but, well, it was very sad, he was too young to go really, only in his forties," And then quickly, "I've had a boyfriend since, but he lives in America now. He's got a good job in New York."

Before he could reply, before he could say once again that he was sorry, I said, "And you? Are you married?"

He shook his head, tiny little shakes, "No, I was but…" He hesitated but then said, "Any children?"

"Yes, a daughter, oh, and a granddaughter now. She's only four months old. You?"

"No, but…"

"But?" The door pinged, and a large group of young women sauntered inside, laughing and chattering in excited, high-pitched voices, so I had to lean closer to hear him. The coffee machine whooshed again, and the piped music became louder. I recognized it, the yearning soaring nostalgia of Barry White's *"Love's Theme."*

He hung his head, staring at the red and white checked tablecloth, seeming fascinated by his plate, his empty cup, as he spoke, "No, um, we're divorced. I spent too much time searching for somebody." He said this very quietly, and as he looked up, our gazes met, his eyes green and wet as moss as if he could burst into tears. I don't know why, but I snaked my hand across the table to touch his. He grabbed it tightly as if it were a lifeline, saying, "I'm sorry, I don't usually talk about it, but..."

"You don't need to talk about it if you can't or don't want to," I said softly.

"Oh, I do," he replied, "I've carried it for so long," He shook his head, staring into space, "I suppose I'm weary." He stopped for a second and took a deep breath, "You see," He fixed his gaze full on me, "I feel I've been searching for her all my life."

Puzzled, I frowned and, shaking my head slightly, said, "Who?"

"My daughter," he replied, and when I looked at him, frowning, not understanding, "She went missing a long time ago, years ago."

"I'm so sorry," and then glancing around, "From here, Hebden Bridge, I mean?"

He shook his head as he took his hands from mine and searched through his pockets for a tissue that he used to blow his nose, "No, from Todmorden. I lived there then."

"I grew up in Todmorden," I told him as I waved to the waitress and asked for more drinks for both of us.

He shrugged, "Well, you may remember it then. It was a very high-profile case." He spread his hands and widened his eyes, "In all the papers, on the TV, the radio. She went missing from her nursery."

"Her nursery? Oh my God!" The waitress bustled to the table with steaming pots of tea and coffee, clean cups, and saucers. We nodded our thanks as I poured the scalding liquid and Andy pulled his chair closer to mine and kept on talking, all the hurts and disappointments he'd endured over the years pouring out in a torrent. A fast-raging torrent that I thought would never stop.

CHAPTER TWO

Nineteen-Ninety

That wasn't really what I wanted to do when I left school when I had passed all my exams with flying colors and would be untethered to roam the world as I wished, maybe to float like a balloon high up in the sky, dodging amongst the clouds. I hadn't wanted to float, though. I wanted to make my mark; I wanted to write eventually, be a real author, so when I was gone, there would be published books left behind, all my written words for everyone to read for years and years to come, so I would never be forgotten. Ha, the silly aspirations of a sixteen-year-old, right?

"Jenny, you can't go out into the world with just your qualifications," I'd been told by our "Career's Advisor," a woman who looked like a child, who looked almost as young as me, far too young to be a working adult, with her long dark hair tied up in a neat ponytail, her face free of make-up.

"But why, Miss?"

"You'll need to train. Girls like you usually go to beauty college to train as a hairdresser or secretarial college to train as a secretary. It's just another string to your bow, something to fall back on."

"But I want to be a writer, Miss."

She'd looked doubtful, "You'd have to be really good at English to become a writer, but if your exam results are good, maybe one day. For now, though, I'd suggest secretarial college for you. You'll be taught to touch type, a skill we mustn't lose, to answer phone calls in a business-like manner, to file papers. You'll also get training in computers." I remember her gazing at me, her eyes narrowed, "In fact, you may even get a job in a legal setting, a solicitor's office, for example. In the meantime, I have a work experience for you."

Grinning, I said, "Oh wow, Miss, where?"

"In *"Toddy Tots Day Nursery."*

"In a day nursery? But, Miss …"

"It's only for two weeks, Jenny, and you'll get your all-important introduction to the working world. You'll get experience in following orders, interaction with work colleagues, and, most importantly, confidence. Confidence to pursue other avenues in your life. Do you understand?"

"Yes, Miss," I remembered saying doubtfully. So that was why I was there in *"Toddy Tots Day Nursery."*

It was my first day, and the supervisor, Vanessa Lynch, a woman of at least thirty with an amazing cloud of frizzy hair, was introducing me to the children. There were twenty of them, their ages ranging from two years old to four, their faces expectant, staring from the teacher back to me, all sitting cross-legged in rows on the floor.

Vaness had pointed out each child, painstakingly slowly, until I thought we'd never get through them all but, nearing the end now, she said, "And right at the back, there's Bobby, Lucy, oh and Susie, last but by no means least."

Susie became one of my favorites, a quiet little girl but confidently coming out of her shell once you got to know her. I remembered that day, the day it happened. She wore her long golden hair in waves, some of it pulled up away from her face and tied in a bright red bow. She had very green eyes set in a heart-shaped face, and that day, she wore a pretty flowered dress, poppies, I think they were a white cardigan over the top and frilly ankle socks. Her name suited her too, Susie."

"Susie, put the kettle on, Susie, put the kettle on, we'll all have tea, we'll all have tea."

"It's Suki," I remember telling her, "Suki put the kettle on."

Cheekily, she'd put out her tongue, "No, Miss,

it's Susie, it really is!"

"My name's Susan, really," I remember her telling me, "But Mummy and Daddy always call me Susie."

We spent some of the day painting in an arts and crafts session. She was making a Father's Day card for her daddy, so it must have been June. Wasn't Father's Day always in June? She'd drawn him with a large head covered in dark hair, green eyes just like hers, an oblong body, and long, spindly legs. She concentrated, the tip of her tongue showing between her lips.

"Daddy looks cool," I said, and I remember she'd laughed in delight, her green eyes sparkling, saying over and over again, "Daddy Cool, Daddy Cool."

"Mummy has a baby in her tummy," she said in a matter-of-fact way, "It's a sister for me."

"Wow, you're so lucky," I'd said, "Is there a name for her?"

"Tracy, Mummy said, but," She came closer and whispered, "We like it, Mummy and me, but Daddy doesn't."

"No? What name does Daddy want then?"

"Mona," she'd said smartly.

"Mona?"

"Yep," she'd replied, as she colored even more green into Daddy's eyes, "He loves that name."

I recall we laughed long and hard, Vanessa looking on, pleased I could tell that I was bonding so well with the children. Maybe this was my calling, to work with children? For just that one day, any thoughts of secretarial college and becoming a writer went out of my head. "Children," I remember thinking, "Working with children is so cool."

With Vanessa's permission, I left early that night, I think I had a dental appointment, or was it the doctor? I'm not sure now, not after all the years that had flowed seamlessly by changing my memories and altering my perspective. All I know is that when I arrived at *"Toddy Tots Day Nursery,"* the following morning, Susie wasn't there, nor the next nor the next. In fact, and it still hurts my heart, I never saw Susie Valentine ever again.

***

Present Day

"Dave seems to be having a ball in New York," I told Emma as we strolled along the towpath, Emma pushing baby Milly, who slept like an angel in her pram. I peered in, relishing the sight of her beautiful sleeping face framed by a mop of thick black hair, reminding me so much of Emma as a baby that it seemed untrue. As if she'd been cloned or I'd gone back in time. I gazed at Emma, then at her shiny dark hair cut in a smart bob, her lips colored with her trademark red lipstick, shaped like a little bow. She looked fit and slim, for someone who'd had a baby only four months ago, in her black leggings and long red top, multi-colored trainers on her feet.

My mind raced back over the years, realizing it didn't seem two minutes since it was me pushing the pram, baby Emma inside, as I walked alongside this very canal, the Rochdale Canal, but the Todmorden end and not the Hebden Bridge end as we were now. The long walks every day had helped me so much with the battle of the baby blues, not to mention losing all the baby weight. Emma's voice cut into my thoughts, "Yeah, well, I didn't really say this before, Mum, I suppose I didn't want to hurt you, but I'm glad Dave's gone."

"You are? But why?" I gazed at her, open mouthed, and stopped mid-stride. People grumbled as they tried to walk around me, cyclists dinging their bells and runners puffing and panting, dragging their feet.

"Well," She shrugged and gave me an annoyed stare, "Oh, I knew you didn't realize, Mum."

"Realize what?" I was totally mystified.

We started to walk again, slowly, Emma pushing the pram, as she said, "I thought he bullied you. Actually, I'm surprised you didn't give in to the pressure and go to America with him."

"I wouldn't do that. I wanted to be here with you, and Jack, and baby Milly, of course."

"Yeah, he hated the time you spent with me, didn't he? He's a typical narcissist."

"Really?"

The baby stirred a little and began to grizzle, "Hey, Mum, can we just sit here for a minute or two?" She pointed to a bench and, bringing the pram to a stop, sat down, rocking it gently, hoping to soothe Milly. Sitting down next to her, I gazed idly at the brown waters of the canal, watching quacking ducks, their tiny legs moving quickly as they swam alongside swans and geese. I watched leaves falling slowly from the trees, twirling and swirling through the air before landing on the water and floating lazily in their wake.

A group of chattering birds came to walk flat-footed on the towpath, begging for scraps or pecking pieces of ice cream cornet from the ground bought from the nearby vendor. The weather had improved as the day passed by, and the sky was blue now, the sun having burned all the clouds away.

"Did you hear what I said, Mum? Dave acted like a typical narcissist."

"I don't think I realized," I replied, "Okay, he could be bossy, but I didn't always take any notice."

"I've seen a lot more of you since he left," she

said, "I feel that I've got my mum back. Jack thought the same. Oh, and it's not because he's not my real dad or anything like that. Actually, I was glad, at first, when you met someone after Dad died. I didn't want you to be on your own."

I smiled and patted her hand, "I know. How is Jack, anyway?"

"Oh, really cool."

"Doing well at work?"

"Oh yeah, he got a raise, you know."

I glanced at her, "Really?"

"Yeah, so we're," She blushed a little, "Um, thinking of maybe trying for a brother or sister for Milly. We can afford it now." I smiled and squeezed her arm just as her phone buzzed, and she quickly dug inside her bag to retrieve it.

"His ears must have been burning," She waved her phone, "A text from Jack." She replied straight away, her thumbs tapping out a message at lightning speed. I was always amazed that, after all these years, I could still type fast and furious on a great hulking manual typewriter, yet could only painstakingly peck out a message with one finger on a mobile phone. This thumbed way of messaging, so easy for Emma, was beyond me.

Milly totally soothed now, we stood up and resumed our walk, Emma going back to the subject of Dave. “Whatever I’ve said about Dave, though, Mum, his leaving seems to have really upset you. You haven’t even had your hair cut since.” She gave me a side eyed glance, saying quickly, “I hope that hasn’t offended you.”

“No, of course not. I know it needs doing and that I look a fright.”

“I didn’t say that,” she shot back at me, “It’s just…”

“Yeah, I know, but do you know what, Emma?”

“What?” We’d arrived at my boat, so we stopped and Emma carefully handed Milly to me as she dealt with the pram, collapsing it into a small cube so we could store it on the deck. Milly moved sleepily in my arms, so bringing her gently to my shoulder, I kissed her soft cheek, inhaling that lovely baby smell of milk and powder.

“Go on, Mum, tell me,” Emma urged once we were sitting in the boat, the kettle purring away, and mugs ready with instant coffee, milk, and sugar, and Milly sucking contentedly on a bottle.

“Oh, it’s nothing,” I said, reluctant now to tell her about Andy Valentine. Sydney appeared from the bedroom and, jumping onto my lap, curled into a ball and promptly went to sleep.

“Mum?”

I kept my eyes down, so intent was I on stroking

the cat, "Okay. It's just that, fright that I am, a man flirted with me the other day."

She looked up from Milly, her eyes and mouth surprised "O's" in her face, "Oh yeah, flirted, eh?" She narrowed her eyes as if she was laughing at me.

Smiling, I met her gaze, "It's true. His name is Andy Valentine and he has a large white dog that he calls Ziggy Stardust."

"Andy Valentine? I think he's telling porkies, Mum! Trying to appeal to your romantic side. I mean, who could possibly have the surname Valentine?"

"You'd be surprised," I said as, carefully moving Sydney from my lap, I went into the kitchen just as the kettle boiled. I poured water into our mugs and a dash of milk, "Sugar?"

"Just one, please." I put the steaming mug on the table beside her as I said, "Anthony Valentine, for one."

"Who's that?"

"He was an English actor. I think he died a few years ago, and there's an American actress called Karen Valentine. Oh, and Kathy Valentine was a member of the band the *"Go Go's."*

"Okay, okay," I stand corrected. Milly made soft, sated noises as she finished her bottle and Emma put her onto her shoulder and began to circle her back with the palm of her hand.

"So, when are you going on a date?"

Taking a sip of my drink, I winced as the hot coffee burned my lip, "I don't know, there may not even be one. He's quite troubled, you see. He's searching for his daughter."

Frowning, she asked, "Where's she gone?"

"Well, that's the problem, he doesn't know. She's been missing since she was a four-year-old child, since nineteen ninety in fact."

"Oh my God," Emma looked at me, her face distraught, "That's terrible. She'll be in her thirties now." She gazed at Milly, who, laying on her back, slept peacefully in her arms, "I couldn't bear to lose Milly, and she's only four *months* old."

I nodded, "I know and the sad thing is that, well, I remember her."

"What?"

"Yes, I was sixteen and worked for a time at the nursery she went to. The trouble is, Emma, I was hoping I could help him, but everything that happened at the time is pretty hazy."

"Mum, if she hasn't been found after all these years, how do you think you can help him?"

Sadly, I shook my head, "I know, I suppose I'm being silly. But there's something, a memory, I can't explain it, Emma. Maybe I've blocked it out."

Emma shrugged, "There's people that can help,

that can unblock memories, but anyway, what about the police? Didn't they question you at the time?"

"Yes," I nodded my head, "The following day, but I had nothing to tell them. I left early the day it happened. It was my first day at the nursery and I had a dental appointment or the doctor, I'm not sure, but I wasn't there at the crucial time."

"So, you didn't see anything when you left the building?"

Slowly, I shook my head, and for some strange reason, I felt a sense of anxiety coming over me, "I don't know, Emma, I really don't, not after all this time. I mean, I've been back there, to the nursery in Todmorden and looked around the area, but nothing comes back to me, nothing at all."

She shrugged, "Well, as I said, Mum, there are people who can help unblock memories. You'll have to google it. There may even be somebody local."

I gazed at her thoughtfully as Emma stood up, "Have you told him, um, Andy, that you remember his daughter?"

Slowly, I shook my head, "No."

"Are you going to tell him?"

I shrugged, "I don't know. I don't know what to do, Emma."

"But you'll be seeing him again? Has he got your number?"

"Yes, we exchanged numbers."

She smiled and said, "Well, I know you'll do the right thing. Look, Mum, I've got to go, I want to walk back."

Carefully taking Milly from her, I said, "It's a long way, at least five miles. I could take you in the car?"

"No, it's okay Mum, I need the exercise," She patted her stomach and grinned.

"There's nothing there," I said, nudging her arm with mine, "I've seen more fat on a lamb chop!"

She giggled as she carefully put Milly in the pram and, turning towards me, gave me a hug. I called after her, "Text when you're safely home, Emma."

She turned and nodded her head, raising her hand in acknowledgement, as I watched her walk away until she was a tiny dot in the distance and then until I couldn't see her at all.

***

Later that evening, my laptop in front of me, a glass of wine at my side, my ongoing book *"Hidden Desires,"* and the paltry few sentences I'd typed so far open on the screen which, promptly, I hid as thoughts of what Emma had said earlier came into my mind, and I tapped into google, *"How to unblock a memory."* An article popped up straight away, an article entitled, *"How traumatic memories hide in the brain, and how to retrieve them,"* my eyes skimmed over the words on the screen, words that talked about the concept of repressed memories that focus on traumatic events that a person may not remember at all, or may not remember until after the event.

Repressed memories being memories that aren't easily accessed consciously. However, the theory of repressed memories is highly controversial and remains unproven. Some experts believe that the brain has varied pathways to protection, including storing memories in ways that may not be completely remembered at all times.

Blinking my eyes away from the screen, I peered through the boat's porthole. It was growing dark now, the canal a thick black line, above which the wide trunks and curly heads of trees could be seen like very large ice cream cones. White blobs of swans swam smoothly with barely a ripple on the water, followed by chattering geese that suddenly took off, forming a vee in the sky that arched overhead, a navy blue speckled with dark fluffy clouds. I took a sip of wine, feeling its warmth travel down my throat and into my stomach.

My eyes returned to the screen, and I carried on reading that it was recommended to consult a licensed therapist or psychologist who specializes in trauma as well as trying various things that may unblock the memories, such as holding an old article of clothing, reading an old letter, diary entry or newspaper article or maybe listening to an old song.

"It's a defense mechanism," I thought to myself, "Humans must have a defense mechanism to protect themselves from the hurt of unwanted memories." There was something, though, hidden at the back of my mind, or perhaps there wasn't, and it was simply that for all the years since that fateful day, I'd thought I should know something but didn't really. Should I speak to Andy Valentine, though, and tell him I'd known his little girl, even if for such a short time? What should I do? Somebody, please tell me.

Sighing, I picked up my phone and, tapping on contacts, scrolled down slowly until I saw Andy's name that I'd put into my phone after our meeting in the café just a few days before. The phone beeped, prompting me with the words, send a text? Decisively, I tapped on yes and, without further hesitation, typed out a hasty one-fingered message to Andy Valentine asking if we could meet.

CHAPTER THREE

Dusk was falling as I made my way through the heart of Hebden Bridge, walking past shops closed up for the night, subdued lighting shining behind their plate glass windows that were sandwiched between bars lit up in cozy orange and red glows. Glancing in, I saw people inside, relaxing after a hard day's work, not a care in the world, sitting in groups or couples in animated conversation, chatting and laughing, a glass at their side and plates of food or crisps and nuts. Cheerful music oozed out onto the street. The air was cold and autumnal for the end of September, mixed with the salty smell of fish and chips and the pungency of curry as it wafted from the local takeaways.

I wasn't used to being outside at this time of night, so I found it fascinating, this world of after-dark, this world of pubs and bars of drinking and music. Gazing at the smiling people inside, living their lives behind the windows like fish in a bowl, I felt left out, an alien, lonely somehow, but walked forward purposefully, confidently so nobody would ever guess, would ever know the truth.

Unsure what to wear for my meeting with Andy, I opted for jeans teamed with trainers and a plain black tee shirt. I'd shrugged on my favorite coat, a cream trench coat that I wore belted tightly at the waist as if it was the nineteen sixties. Even my make-up reflected that era, thick black eye-makeup and pale pink lips, and with my new hairdo, I felt sure I didn't look like a shapeless sack anymore.

My phone buzzed, so I delved into my pocket and pulled it out, gazing at the screen with a frown. A text message, *"Hi, are you okay? On your way?"*

I texted back quickly, *"Yes, I'm almost at the pub."* The public house The Railway came into view, its sign of a puffing green train lit up with a bright white light. He was waiting at the door, a welcoming smile on his face, holding out a hand and saying, "So good to see you again." As we shook, I felt a jolt like electricity going through me just at the touch of his hand. He smiled, the wrinkles around his eyes creasing very attractively. He indicated with his head, "Come inside. What would you like to drink?"

The warmth hit me like a pea-souper of a fog, as well as the loud talking and laughter, the sound of an acoustic guitar trying to break through, as if the sound of merriment was a thick brick wall, "Um, a glass of red wine? Merlot?"

"Coming up." He gave me a cheeky wink, "Do you want to sit over there?" He pointed to some seats in the window, gathered around a small square table decorated interestingly with lozenges of different colored tiles in bright primary colors of red, blue, yellow, and green. People stared, as self-consciously I sat down, smiling and nodding at their interested gazes, and then looked down at the table, fiddling with the beer mat.

A young man with a bushy beard, wearing jeans and a denim jacket, was perched on a stool like a pea on a drum, strumming on a guitar, his voice plaintive, almost sad, becoming stronger and stronger as he tried to compete with the noise. I noticed a couple of posters advertising an Open Mic Night every Wednesday, so I supposed this was it.

"There you are," Andy put a glass of wine on a beer mat and sat down opposite me, nodding and smiling at the people around us as if he knew them. I thanked him with a nod of the head and, leaning forward, whispered, "People stare, don't they."

"Yeah, they're just curious, these are people I know just from coming here. They'll be wondering who you are. I'm always alone, you see. For me, to be with a woman is a big deal." He nodded his head and said quickly, "To them, anyway."

I smiled feeling a blush stain my cheeks as I loosened the belt on my trench coat and slipped it off. Nervously I glanced around, noticing a large old-fashioned jukebox in a corner, its lights flashing.

"Wow," I said, "I haven't seen a jukebox like that for years." Andy laughed, showing even white teeth making my heart clatter harder as I took a sip of wine to steady it. "Yeah, it's great. Brilliant songs from the seventies and eighties on there, and the sixties too."

"Oh, I love the sixties."

He sat back in his seat, then stared at me, narrowing his eyes in a most attractive way, "I thought you did; you look very sixties tonight. I like your style, and your hair looks nice."

"Thank you," I felt a hot red blush staining my cheeks, so I quickly changed the subject, "Is T-Rex on the jukebox?"

"Yes, of course. 20th Century Boy, Jeepster, Hot Love, they're all there," He leaned closer to me, "The other night, somebody put on Puppy Love by Donny Osmond. I think it was one of the local football teams. A big guy with a shaven head and tattoos."

"How did you know it was him?"

"The whole team sang along," He gave me a knowing nod of the head and a crafty wink, "A dead giveaway, really." He took a sip from his pint glass, leaving foam on his lip, which he flicked away with his tongue, making my heart clatter even harder.

I laughed in delight, "No! I haven't heard that song for ages, and I really can't imagine the man you described liking that song."

Andy laughed, "I know, to say I was surprised is an understatement, but as they say there's nowt queerer than folk," He shook his head sadly, "You just don't get songs like that anymore. My sister loved it."

I laughed and said, "That's a very Yorkshire saying," and then, "Yeah, well, so did I," nostalgia overwhelmed me at the thought of my teenage love for Donny Osmond. I took another sip of wine, liking the warm, soothing feeling as it shot through my body, easing the knots in my stomach that I hadn't really realized were there.

"You mean like, "Eye up, your brew's mashin'?"

I laughed, "Yes, that's right, my dad was very fond of making a brew."

"Your parents? Have you…?"

"No," I shook my head, feeling the familiar tightening in my throat when I spoke of my parents, "Unfortunately not, you?"

"No, I'm an orphan too, which I don't suppose is so surprising at our ages."

There was a short silence, which Andy broke by saying, "Anyway," He leaned forward, his elbows on the table. He wore jeans and a white shirt open at the neck, showing an expanse of chest hair, over which he wore a long black overcoat. The stubble on his cheeks and chin was thick and black, making him look even more rugged and desirable. I tried to avert my gaze, which was very difficult when he was sitting right there in front of me, "How come you're living on a boat in Hebden Bridge?"

"When my boyfriend and I split up, we sold our house in Todmorden, so I decided to see what it was like living on a boat," I shrugged, "A nice change, I thought."

He nodded, leaning in closer as the acoustic guitar finished for now. The jukebox suddenly burst out with the opening bars of *"Mr. Blue Sky."* We stared at each other and smiled, "ELO, brilliant band," he said, and then, "Yeah, go on. Your boyfriend's gone to America, though, is that right?"

I nodded, "Yes. I didn't want to go. My daughter was heavily pregnant at the time. I have a granddaughter now," He nodded with understanding.

He sipped again at his pint as *"Mr. Blue Sky"* finished, and the Osmonds started singing *"Crazy Horses."*

"Oh my God, what a fabulous jukebox."

He nodded and said, "I told you so," as I carried on, "I'm not sure if I'll live on the boat for long, though."

"Why?"

"Well, it depends on what it's like in the dead of winter when I have to go outside to fetch water and fuel for the stove." He gave a snort of laughter, "I'm not sure how cold it's going to get; the canal might freeze. It's a fairly old boat from the seventies, so I need to get it checked out within the next couple of weeks or so, make sure the roof is tight and the boiler is okay."

He nodded and took another sip of beer, "Yeah, I see what you mean. I suppose we all have a romantic vision of what it could be like, and maybe it is in the summer."

"Oh yeah, it's been great so far. I've lived there for four months now, but it's the end of September, and the nights are drawing in."

"Don't people just cruise in the winter?"

"Yeah, some do, but that can be fraught with difficulties because of two things," I ticked them off on my fingers, "Once again, ice and stoppages."

"Stoppages?"

"Yeah, some sections of the canal can be closed for essential winter maintenance."

He smiled and shook his head, "I see what you mean. Narrow boating is definitely not just plain sailing. Oh, and pardon the pun." We laughed as Andy carried on, "How come your boyfriend didn't just stay with you. I can't imagine taking off like that and leaving you alone with a grandchild on the way as well."

I shrugged, "It's a great opportunity for him, and he loves living in New York. I didn't want to stand in his way, and we weren't married, so there was nothing holding him back, really."

My voice drained away as Andy said, "Yeah, each to his own, I suppose, but I don't know if I could swap New York for the beauty of Hebden Bridge."

"I know, there's a vast difference, but apparently Central Park has its benefits." I smiled and drained my wine, going to my bag, ready to go to the bar.

"No, please, let me, Jenny."

Before I could resist, he got up, taking our glasses with him as he walked to the bar, chatting and nodding to people as he went. A group of bearded, long-haired men came to sit at the table next to ours, dressed in denim and leather like a biker gang. They made a racket, scraping their chairs on the floor and bantering with each other in loud voices. The jukebox suddenly stopped mid-song, and another man, slightly older this time, holding tightly to a guitar, took center stage on the bar stool. Everybody quietened down this time as he began to strum and to sing with a surprisingly good voice.

"One of the locals," whispered Andy as he came back from the bar and sat down next to me this time, his thigh straining against the material of his jeans, brushing mine. "He's very well thought of."

"He's very good," I said quietly.

Everybody seemed intent on the singer for a while with a respectful silence, and then a slight murmuring rose up again, prompting Andy to lean in close to me and say, "Why did you want to meet tonight, Jenny? Have you something you want to talk about?"

"Yes," I sighed, realizing our conversation so far had just been idle chit-chat, Andy probably waiting with bated breath for me to speak to tell him why I'd wanted us to meet. "I don't know whether or not I can help you, but," I took a deep breath, "Well, the thing is, I remember your little girl, Susie."

With a look of bewilderment on his face, he said, "How?"

"I was doing my work experience in *"Toddy Tots Day Nursery."*

"Wow," He stared at me, mouth agape, "Were you questioned by the police?"

"Yes, but I had nothing to tell them. I left early that day, my first day, but something rankles, Andy, I have something in my mind that just won't take shape."

He took a glug of beer, looking at me over the top of his pint glass, his gaze narrowed, as he shrugged and shook his head, "It's been a long time, Jenny, thirty-three years, even if you do remember something, Susie is gone."

"Not necessarily, Andy. Isn't there always hope?"

He gave a dry chuckle, "My heart tells me yes, but my head tells me no." He reached for my hand and squeezed it hard, "But thanks for telling me."

"Andy!"

"Look, Jenny," He put his pint on the table and turned his upper body towards me, "I've been searching for Susie for every single minute of those years, and there's been nothing. It's as if she disappeared into thin air. I've followed so many leads and been disappointed every time. I don't know if I can do it again. Even the police have written it off after so many years. It's a cold case."

I felt a pang as I gazed at him, thinking of his life and how it had been ruined really, how he was living on a knife edge, searching day after day, his marriage fading away like ice on a summer day, no new relationship and no more children, as far as I was aware, and what did I have to offer him? The fact that I'd spoken only once to his daughter and just a hunch, something that hovered at the back of my mind, something I thought I saw? It wasn't enough, really, was it?"

"I'm sorry, Andy. There's not enough to go on

at the moment, is there?"

He drained his pint and began to stand up, "Come on, Jenny, I'll walk you home."

I felt a plummeting in my stomach at the thought he was cutting the evening short, and I took a last sip of wine before shrugging on my coat and standing up, tying the belt tight at the waist. "I have to be up early for work tomorrow, Jenny," he whispered close, his breath tickling my ear, "So I'm not cutting the evening short or anything like that."

I nodded as I was followed by people's stares. We left the pub and made our way down the main street lit up by pools of orange that glowed from the street lights. *"The Old Gate"* pub looked like a fairyland; all the tiny white lights draped around the outside seating area twinkling as we walked past. It was a still night without a breath of wind and cold now, the pitch-black sky arched above set with millions of tiny stars and the moon a bright white glow hanging like a lantern.

"Where do you work?" I asked him as we strolled along, Andy, shoulders hunched to his ears, his hands pushed down into his pockets.

"I'm on the council," he said with a grin, "Hebden Royd Town Council. I'm the Deputy Clerk."

"Wow, what an interesting-sounding job."

"Yeah, it has it's up's and down's. Working with Councilors can be difficult," He gave me a sideways glance, "Have you still got writer's block?"

"I've had a tiny unblockage," I said with a smile, "I've actually written half a chapter."

He smiled at me, wrinkles forming around his eyes in a most becoming way, "Brilliant. I'm glad for you. It must be frustrating when that happens."

We walked down a couple of deep stone steps, worn smooth by countless walking boots, onto the towpath where the local wildlife seemed to be settling down for the night as ducks and geese stood quietly, their tiny heads nestled into their wings. The ghostly white shapes of swans still swam slowly on the black water. My boat loomed into view, and we came to a stop outside.

Andy put out a hand and cupped my elbow, "I've enjoyed tonight, Jenny, thank you." Leaning forward, his lips brushed my cheek. He smelt good of soap and beer, even a whiff of cigarette smoke, which was warm and comforting, and I longed to press myself close against him and put my lips against his, but I moved away, searching in my bag for the door key. He stood waiting while I clambered onto the deck and unlocked the door, a segment of bright white light pooling out from the lamp I'd left on inside, showing tiny flies and insects hovering in the air.

"Take care, Jenny."

"Goodbye, Andy."

I peered through the window as he turned and walked back towards the town. Was he going straight home or back to the Railway for another drink? Maybe his friends in there would ask where I was. I imagined their questions, "Where's that woman, eh, Andy?"

"Oh, I dropped her off at home, not a long walk. She lives on a boat, you know."

"Not keen then?"

I imagined him shrugging and saying, "Well, a bit of a let-down tonight, I'm afraid," as he ordered a pint and went to sit with his buddies to enjoy what remained of the evening.

Shrugging off my trench coat, I hung it in the cupboard and, fetching a bottle of red, poured myself a glass and sipped it, annoyed with myself for jumping in on his grief like that. After all, what did I possibly think I could do. His child had been missing for thirty-three years, and I thought I could step in and put it all right. What a fool I was. I very much doubted I would be asked to have further cozy chats over a coffee or a wine with Andy Valentine.

Sydney suddenly appeared and, purring like a little motor, jumped up onto my lap, digging into me with her paws as if she were making a bed. Isn't that what cats were supposed to be doing when they did that? Making a bed? Or was it kneading dough? I knew it was one or the other. Eventually, she stopped and, turning around and around in circles a few times, settled into a warm, pulsating ball.

"Well, Sydney," I said, as I stroked her soft fur from the tip of her ears to the top of her tail, "It's just you and me now. No more Dave (and there was a certain amount of relief there) and no more Andy Valentine (no relief there, but, well, there hadn't been time yet, had there?)

Sighing deeply, I sipped at my wine, feeling its fruitiness rushing through my body and yet somehow straight to my head. It intrigued me that any alcoholic liquid a person swallowed went downwards yet invariably ended up affecting the head more than anywhere else. Just one of those weird things, I suppose. My eyes started to fail me, and feeling too sleepy to stay awake any longer, I locked up and, switching off the lamps, made my groggy way to bed.

CHAPTER FOUR

Present Days – Two Weeks Later

"Dave, really, I must get on, I'm in the middle of writing, and I've only just managed to get rid of that pesky writer's block …"

"Ah, writing another "Desire" novel, are you?"

"Well, yes, I am, but you know I don't like discussing my work with anyone when I'm writing it."

"You and your spicy novels, Jenny. I've told all my new buddies here about you, and they'd love to have a meet, you being a famous novelist and all."

"I hardly think I'm famous, Dave, I've got a good publisher but that's as far as it goes. And as for spicy, it's called romance, Dave."

"Stop being so critical of yourself. Bull yourself up. You're a good writer and for people that like spiciness in the written word, or okay romance, you're a great writer." He let out a great bellow of laughter.

Sighing and shaking my head, I really wished

Dave would get off the line. He'd taken to calling me a lot, like three or four times a week, always from his office in New York and always bragging about the view he had and how well he was doing. That he had umpteen new buddies and went regularly to parties and barbeques, for horse-drawn carriage rides in Central Park, regular travel on the Staten Island ferry to the many amazing beaches, and even had groups of close buddies for dinner and drinks in his apartment, which also had panoramic views of New York. It seemed as if Dave's life was one big round of enjoyment. Was I jealous? Well, erm, no, of course not! Well, not much, just a sliver.

"Oh, stop it, Dave," I said, "You sound as if you've got a starring role in that TV program "Friends." This was followed by another great bellow of laughter and then, "Hey, Jenny, look out for me. In a few months, maybe January or February, I'm gonna make a surprise visit to Hebden."

"No, Dave, really, you know I don't like surprises. Let me know if you're coming over for a visit. I can arrange accommodation for you. There's some lovely little B&Bs around here."

"What, no room on the boat?"

"Dave!"

There was a brief cackle of laughter and then, "Nah, I'm gonna surprise you, maybe even for

Valentine's."

"Dave, Valentine's Day is just one big hype, so please, no surprises." And then, as per usual, "Hey, my office phone's ringing sweetheart, I gotta go," and suddenly he was gone, and with relief, I could click off my mobile and put it safely back in my pocket. Emma's comment about Dave being a narcissist flashed through my mind. Maybe she was on to something there, something that had always been there and I'd not even noticed.

My concentration was broken, I tried to get back into my writing, but too late, the thread had gone, so invariably, my thoughts would wander to Andy Valentine. Well, the lack of Andy Valentine. There'd been no word from him since our drink in The Railway pub two weeks ago. Did you see that? Read it properly, did you? Yes, two weeks ago! It was the evening I told him I remembered his little girl, Susie. Since that time, I'd thought of him constantly, Dave now becoming an irritation whereas before meeting Andy, I'd really thought I'd missed him.

Andy was the reason that I now had a compulsion to constantly check my phone for texts just in case, and I was always peering out of the boat's tiny porthole window for a glimpse of him walking his big fluffy dog, Ziggy Stardust along the towpath, or maybe I should say shuffling his way along through the golden autumn leaves. It seemed he'd disappeared into thin air, well, from any air around me at any case. What dreary company I must have been that night, that's for sure, and that, I thought with a heavy heart, was in spite of going all out and braving the hairdresser for a new hairdo.

My eyes sought the screen of my laptop again, and I began to read through Jeanette and Josh's latest exploits (yes, I'd changed the hero's name from Henry to Josh). The name Josh came across just that bit sexier, really, and that's only personal preference. I'm pretty sure there are men called Henry who are extremely sexy. In fact, there's not one single reason in the world why a man called Henry can't be sexy, but, hmm, I'm digging a hole here. Sorry, men called Henry; I hope you're not offended. I'm going to stop now! Yes, Jenny, stop!

My phone started buzzing, so quickly I pulled it from my pocket, "Hello?"

"Hi, Mum, it's only me."

"Emma! How are you?"

"I'm fine. Would you do me a favor?"

"Of course. When do you want me to look after my sweet granddaughter."

"Well, it's not babysitting, Mum. Would you come with me to a council meeting tonight?"

"A council meeting? Tonight? But…"

"Just hear me out, okay. I've got to speak, Mum, and I'm so nervous."

"Speak about what, Emma?"

"Do you remember when we moved into our house, and the farmer that owned the field behind us promised he'd never sell for building?"

"Yes, I think so."

"Well, even though we had verbal assurance that he wouldn't sell, and he even signed a document promising that very thing, he's gone ahead and sold to a builder, and everybody's up in arms. We've been offered a slot at the council meeting tonight to air our views. The farmer's going to be there as well."

"What are they planning to build on the land?"

"Four detached dwellings. Oh Mum, please come with me. I really need some support. The meetings in Hebden Bridge at the council offices there, not in Tod, so it's easy for you to get to.

"Well, yes, of course I will. Shall I meet you there?"

"Thanks, Mum, yes, the meeting starts at seven. See you there."

I clicked off my phone, feeling strangely elated that Emma wanted me there. Even at her age, in her thirties, she still needed her mum. I hummed a little tune whilst turning back to my laptop and once again reading through what I'd written earlier, "Okay,

Jeanette and Josh," I said to the laptop, "Let's have some real action."

***

The Council Chamber in Hebden Royd Council offices was packed when Emma and I walked in that evening. A group of women, who I assumed must be her neighbors, immediately raised their arms, beckoning her over to sit with them.

"This is my mum," she said as she introduced me, "Jenny Clarke. She's come to give us moral support.

They all nodded respectfully as if, because of age, I was the matriarch of the group as Emma introduced each of them, saying, "This is Lilly, and there's Poppy, Daisy's over there," after the third flower name I zoned out a bit and just smiled politely and nodded. I can't remember the other names too well, but one was similar to a car, Mercedes maybe, and the other some sort of white wine, no, not Liebfraumilch, but something similar. Once the business of names was over, I gazed around, noticing how much like a courtroom this place was with its dark paneled walls and stately looking chairs raised up above the ordinary seating below that was for us, the common folk, the largest and most ornate of which the mayor now sat on.

Idly, I glanced at the name placard in front of him, *Councilor Ronald Rudd, Town Mayor.* The chair next to his was occupied by a large, stern-looking woman whose placard said, *"Mrs. Linda Ogilvie, Town Clerk.* The seat next to her was empty, although there was a placard there that read… oh good God, *Mr. Andy Valentine, Deputy Town Clerk,* why didn't I think of that before! I just didn't connect the two, the council meeting and the Deputy Clerk!

Oh no, where was he? Was he here? A figure suddenly swept across my vision, and there he was just about to sit down when he spied me too and smiled, the wrinkles around his eyes appearing as if by magic. He mouthed across, "Hi Jenny," so politely I inclined my head and smiled back, wondering how somebody could act so normal and nice and yet not have contacted me at all for a whole two weeks as if I'd done something wrong or had hurt them in some way. Hmm, I wondered for the millionth time what thoughts were bubbling away in that handsome head of his.

He looked good, though, wearing a smart striped suit with a white shirt and a tie, and I could see his long black overcoat hanging over the back of his chair. There were several piles of important-looking papers towering in front of him, and the few councilors that were milling around kept stopping to talk, asking questions, and signing documents, making him look even more busy and important than anybody else, until quite suddenly, the mayor banged a gavel and demanded, "Order, please."

The formal business of the council was carried out first with a lot of discussion about various minutes, and there was a lot of hand raising and, yes, councilor, no councilor. The mayor signed a lot of papers, which he immediately handed to the Clerk, who immediately handed them over to the Deputy Clerk, who added them to the pile of papers already in front of him. Andy's expression stayed smooth and calm as I watched him add to the ever-increasing "filing."

After what seemed like hours, I felt Emma tense beside me as the mayor began to talk about a local planning issue that had been referred to the Planning Committee, a misunderstanding, as he referred to it, between a local man, Farmer Giles (really?) and several homeowners at Bush Row in Todmorden. This was met with an irate nudge from the Clerk who, leaning in close, whispered in the mayor's ear.

"Oh, I do apologize," said the red-faced mayor, peering at the open-mouthed councilors over the top of his glasses, "I seem to have got a name wrong. It's Farmer Ronald Ormondroyd and not Farmer Giles at all. Sorry about that." There was loud guffaws and titters from the council as the Clerk leaned in again to whisper in his ear, "Oh, and it's Brush Row in Todmorden and not Bush."

He turned to the Clerk, "Thank you for that." Andy's face was impassive despite the detection of a tiny shake of his head and the slow closing of his eyes, whilst, for some reason, the words of a song, *"I am a cider drinker…"* kept going around and around my head.

The mayor's voice broke into my thoughts, "And now, without further ado, I'd like to welcome Mrs. Emma Hudson to the stand. She will be speaking on behalf of all the concerned neighbors on Brush Row. Mrs. Hudson, please."

Emma, red-faced, stood up and, after a brief sideways glance at me, made her way to the stand, where she greeted everybody in a somewhat shaky voice, to begin with, but went on to explain the issue confidently and well. Her speech was met with a smattering of applause from the councilors and wild cheering from her neighbors as, with a dignified nod of her head, she returned to her seat.

"Was I okay?" she whispered as she nudged me with her elbow.

"Brilliant," I whispered back, "Very confident," She smiled happily as the mayor's voice rang out again, "Thank you Mrs. Hudson. Very well put. And now we'd like to welcome Farmer Ronald Giles to the stand." He must have felt the Clerk's menacing stare because he backtracked and stammered, whilst glancing nervously at the notes in front of him, "Oh, sorry, Farmer Ronald *Ormondroyd,* to the stand, please. Thank you." This was met with another round of cheering from the Councilors.

A small grey-haired man, very slope-shouldered and wearing a dusty-looking black suit that was so big on him, you'd think it belonged to his dad or older brother, an off-white open necked shirt and a straw hat, made his way to the stand amidst a sprinkling of clapping from the members of the Planning Committee. He gave a respectful bow of his head, removing his hat and holding it with a tight fist at his heart as if it were his personal talisman before launching confidently into his spiel.

"Thank you for giving me this platform tonight to explain my case. I just have one thing to say, and that is, yes, I sold my land despite saying I wouldn't and despite signing a document to prevent me from doing this. I'm sorry to disappoint the homeowners whose view is my fault, but, well, to put it bluntly, I'm skint and ran out of money. It was the lockdown back in 2020 what started it. Put most of us farmers on the poverty line it did. I had no choice but to sell."

He paused here and gazed around at all the faces that stared at him as if in wonder, *"When that builder approached me, well, I almost bit his hand off so desperate I was and still am, in fact, for the money."* He stopped again and looked towards us, towards Emma and her neighbors. His gaze was open and honest, his washed-out blue eyes candid, *"I don't know what else to say, except that the land is sold and the building will commence, but respectfully, the houses will be built as far from your boundary line as is possible. You're entitled to sue me if that's the road you want to take. Thank you."*

He shuffled away then to a deafening applause from the councilors and a brief shell-shocked response from Emma and her neighbors until they too began to clap, a long, slow clapping as the farmer, ignoring his seat completely, took his leave, the vast oak doors of the Council Chamber swinging shut behind him. The meeting finished not long after that, and Emma and I, surrounded by her neighbors, shuffled in the crowds from the council chamber and along various corridors until we found ourselves outside the building. It was dark now, and the air still and cool, the sky arching above us, a velvety black set with tiny stars and a sliver of a pock-faced moon.

"How could we sue him?" said one of the neighbors, Daisy, I think, "I felt sorry for the poor old chap."

"Yeah, that lockdown! It was hard for everyone but particularly for farmers."

"Farmers have a hard life anyway," said the neighbor, who was named after a bottle of white wine, "My grandad was a farmer, run him into the ground it did."

"Yes," said Emma, "We'll just have to put up with the building work, I'm afraid, and the partial loss of a view after the work is done."

Everybody nodded and agreed and began to peel away back to their cars for the short drive back to Todmorden. I started to walk away with Emma when I heard a voice calling for me and stopped and turned around, "Jenny. Hey, Jenny. Wait a minute, will you?"

I smiled and said, "Hi," as a very breathless Andy Valentine came running towards me, his long black coat flying out behind him.

"Sorry about that," he said, looking from me to Emma and back again, "Quite a defeat, I'm afraid, eh?"

"Oh Andy, this is Emma, my daughter, Emma, this is Andy Valentine."

Emma nodded, "Yeah." She shrugged. "But there's no way we're going to sue him. Oh, pleased to meet you." They shook hands, "You were at the meeting, weren't you?"

Andy nodded, "Yes, I'm the Deputy Clerk," and then, "Pleased to meet you too. I hear what you're saying, but you'd be well within your rights to sue, you know."

"I know, but I think it's the consensus of the group that we wouldn't do that."

Andy nodded slowly and smiled as once again

he looked from one of us to the other, "You look very much alike."

Emma and I exchanged glances and grinned, Emma saying, "Yeah, we've been told that before."

I said, "Well, it's been nice to see you, Andy, but I must get on."

"Um, Jenny, would it be possible to have a quick word?"

"Yes, of course." I gazed towards him, waiting for him to speak.

He blushed a little and said, "I mean, um, alone."

He eyed Emma, who said quickly, "Oh, of course. Sorry." And turning to me, "Mum, I'll ring you tomorrow."

"But Emma…"

"No, please, Mum, go on." She nodded towards Andy with her head, arching her brows as she did so.

"Alright, but ring me when you get home, okay?"

"Yes, I will," and with a grin, "As soon as I walk in the door!"

I watched her as she walked away and then turned back to Andy, feeling a slight twinge of irritation. After all, there'd been two weeks with no contact, and now it was imperative that we talk. What was he up to? "What is it, Andy?"

"Would you like to go for a drink?" He shrugged,

"And a chat?"

"Well, Andy, really, I think, maybe not?"

"Please, Jenny," he interrupted, "I need to explain about the other night." He stared at me hard, his eyes deep and dark as mossy pools. Nervously, he bit his lower lip, leaving it red and swollen as if he'd been kissing. My heart thumped right up into my ears as I thought hard about what I should do. Coming to a decision, I opened my mouth to speak.

CHAPTER FIVE

Present Day

A flurried quacking and honking awoke me the following morning as, groggily, I tried to raise my head from the pillow. A sore head, a head that was suffering from the after-effects of too much red wine, well, too much for a school night anyway. How I'd be able to write today, I'd never know. Perhaps the spicy adventures of Jeanette and Josh would have to be put on hold yet again because, as well as a thumping headache, the words, *"I am a cider drinker, I drinks it all of the day, Ooh, arrh ooh arrh, ay, ooh arrh ooh arrh ay …"* kept running through my head as well as vague thoughts of a Farmer Giles who lived on Bush Row in Todmorden.

Coffee flashed through my mind, hot and rich and thick, and I took a deep breath and tried to sit up, but such a simple task proved far too difficult so, with much sighing, I sank back down and turned over, pulling the quilt snugly around my shoulders, whilst closing my eyes and willing sleep to take me. Oh, take me away, gentle sleep. Lull me in your arms. But it was all to no avail as the noise from outside intensified, and to cap it all, I felt a gentle thud as Sydney jumped up onto the bed and, claws out, began to tap my face.

"No, Sydney, no, please don't, ouch, that hurts," and when she wouldn't stop, I begged her, "Sydney, go and put the kettle on. I need coffee," and her reply? "Meow! I need food, hooman!"

With great resolution, I swung my legs out of bed and stood up, albeit a little shakily. I shrugged on my dressing gown and slipped on fluffy mules and, going to the tiny port hole window, peered out at the crazy antics on the canal with what looked like an all-out war between the ducks and the geese, the great stately swans seeming to take on the role of innocent bystander as they swam serenely amongst them without a care in the world. It was sunny though, the sky blue, water drops flying through the air iridescent against the backdrop of the trees, their leaves a flaming orange and red.

"Hmm," I thought as I flicked on the kettle and put food out for Sydney, her frantic meowing abruptly cut off as she rammed her head into her dish. Relieved, I plonked myself down on the settee, clutching a mug of thick dark coffee, the smell tantalizing, and, as the first sips shot through my veins, everything at last seemed alright with the world. So much so that memories of the evening before started to crash into my mind and I smiled secretly to myself as images of Andy Valentine rose up before me.

I recalled his deep green eyes and luscious red lips and felt again the rasp of his stubble on my cheek as he leaned in to kiss me goodnight. Smiling dreamily, I thought of snippets of our conversation as we'd sat together on high bar stools, our knees touching, soft music echoing all around. Oh, the romance of it all. How easy it would be to write a novel about last night. A real page-turner, and yet all the action was only in my imagination, which was a great pity.

"Ah, you weren't surprised at this turn of events, were you, dear Reader? You knew I'd accept his offer of going for a drink despite the cliffhanger I left for you at the end of the last chapter. Will she or won't she, eh? Did you hazard a guess? I bet you did, lol. Do you know, that's the first time I've used lol? Well, the first time I've used it in the right context. I've used it many times thinking it meant "lots of love" until Emma put me straight and informed me it meant "laugh out loud"! What a fool I am. A laughing stock. Dave was the recipient of many "lots of love" lol's, so I really don't want to make the same mistake with Andy, do I? I don't want him to think I'm coming on too strong by making crazy declarations of love."

Okay, I know you're dying to know, so I'll tell you what happened. Let's go back to last night. Picture us standing outside the Town Hall in Hebden Bridge. Andy huddled into his long black overcoat, holding on with a gloved hand to a shiny leather briefcase, no doubt, holding all his important papers (or, um, filing?), and me wearing my cream trench coat tied in tight at the waist, my hair pulled back from my face showing off my sparkly earrings. Emma was walking away, and I had shouted after her, "Let me know when you're safely home, Emma," or words to that effect.

Andy said, "Can we go for a drink, Jenny?"

"Well, I'm not sure, I..."

"Please, I need to explain about the other night."

There was a long silence where my mind whirred and clicked, and then I said rather primly, "Okay, but just one. It is a school night, after all," which I was going to say all along. I just wanted to keep him guessing. His smile transformed his face, the lovely wrinkles around his eyes showing some serious action, along with the dimples at either side of his mouth, and with his green eyes glowing, his lips like red roses, I was totally captivated. Do you get my drift?

We went to a bar called *"Night Jar,"* a cozy little place with subdued lighting oozing from beneath frilly lampshades, right next door to the picture house where a long queue snaked its way down the street, eager to see the latest blockbuster. We sat at the bar on tall stools, their legs as long and skinny as the dancing girls in the Moulin Rouge.

"I'm sorry, Jenny, about the other night," He took a deep draft of beer, flicking away a bit of stray foam with the tip of his tongue, "I appreciate you telling me you knew Susie and, well, I'm sorry if you felt rebuffed but, well, I've been down so many avenues looking for her ..."

"Andy, it's okay, really," I took a sip of red wine and reveled in the feeling as it shot through my veins like wildfire, "There's not a lot to go on, is there? I met her once at *"Toddy Tots Day Nursery"* when I was sixteen," I shrugged, "That was a long time ago. I'm forty-nine now!"

"Yeah," He stared at me narrow-eyed, "But you said you had a memory and that maybe it could be unblocked?"

I took another sip of wine, my heart clattering, not only because of Andy's presence but because I had a gut feeling that he'd had a change of heart and maybe wanted to pursue my hare-brained scheme now, "Yes, I did say that, but you didn't seem keen, you said you'd searched for so long..."

"I know," He shook his head, "I know what I said, but, well, any lead can only be good. I've thought about it since I last saw you, and I'm willing to give it a try if you are?"

"Oh yes," I told him, "I'm still willing."

"And, well, there's something else, um…" The door opened, letting in a sneaky cool draft followed by a group of young people laughing and chattering, bringing in the smell of curry and fish and chips and the still autumn evening. "The thing is, Jenny, I've had a couple of girlfriends since my wife and I divorced, although it was a long time after, both platonic and romantic, but, well, these women, they don't hang around for long."

Frowning, I gazed at him, "Why?"

"I don't know, they get sick of what they call my "obsession." And when I didn't reply but just looked puzzled, he explained, "The obsession I have about finding my daughter. They get sick of it, and me, and move on, and," He shrugged, "I like you and don't want that to happen this time, so I figured it was best to keep clear of you and in my own silly way, I didn't think to explain that. That's why I didn't contact you."

"Oh, don't worry," I said, crossing my fingers like a schoolgirl, "I'm not looking for romance."

"Oh, right, okay, um, well, that's alright then."

"And, I think it's unfair for anybody to say you have an obsession, you're looking for your daughter, it's bound to take over your life. Anyone would behave in the same way."

"Wow, thank you, Jenny, for that. I'll buy you another drink," He stood up and began to search through his pockets, producing his credit card, which he waved over the bar whilst asking, "Another glass of wine? I know you said you'd only have one, but what do you think?"

I began to fumble in my bag, not daring to look up to meet his gaze, "Did I really say that?"

"Yes, you did. You know, with it being a school night and all." He gave a wry twist of the mouth.

"Well, this is just a one off, so let me get the drinks. It's my turn."

"No, please, you're the only person that's ever understood why I've spent my life searching for Susie and, in my book, that deserves another drink. Wine?"

I nodded, "Yes, please," as the young girl behind the bar began to pour another pint of beer and then opened a small bottle of red wine and, with great flair, emptied it into my glass. Music suddenly started to play, something slow and sexy. Frowning, I said, "I like this, but I can't think what it is..."

Andy put his head to one side as if listening hard, "Ah, Gary Moore, *"Still got the Blues."*" He put my glass of wine on a beer mat.

"Yes, oh yes, I love it."

Andy began to hum and then to sing softly, *"I've*

still got the blues for you…" He gave me a slow smile, wrinkles creasing the corners of his eyes, as he leaned forward and reached for my hand that he squeezed tightly and then abruptly let go leaving my skin warm and tingly, before saying, "Did, um, did Susie say anything to you? Did you have any interaction with her?"

I took a sip of wine, "Oh yes, we had a lovely day. My very first day and, well, she was the star, really. I never forgot her. She told me…um…was your wife pregnant at the time?"

"Yes, she was, but she lost the baby after Susie went missing, the stress, I suppose." He took a deep draft of beer.

"Oh no, I'm sorry."

"No, no, it's fine now, but catastrophic at the time, combined with Susie disappearing, she was about twelve weeks along, so," He let the words hang in the air and then said abruptly, "Did Susie tell you that then, that her mummy was pregnant?"

"Yes, she said mummy had a baby in her tummy and it was a sister for her and that she and mummy wanted to call it Tracy."

His smile lit up his face, "Oh wow, really?"

I nodded, "Yes, but she said that Daddy didn't like the name Tracy and that he wanted to call the baby Mona!"

"Mona?" He threw his head back as he laughed, "Mona?" A sudden spurt of tears welled up, and he frantically tried to blink them away and then padded under his eyes with his fingertips, "Oh, sorry, Jenny, I don't know whether I'm laughing or crying."

"It's okay, really it is. It is funny and sad all at the same time."

Fumbling in his pocket, he pulled out a crumpled tissue, dabbed at his eyes, and then blew his nose, "Do you know, I think she meant Fiona? That's the name I wanted anyway."

"Oh, really? After all this time, I've learned the truth. I always wondered about Mona." We laughed delightedly, and then Andy leaned forward and took both my hands in his, "Thank you for this, Jenny, thank you."

The ringing of my phone brought me out of my reverie, and hastily picking it up, hoping it was Andy, I said, "Hello?"

"Hello, Jenny?"

"Dave?"

"Just checking in. How's things in good old Hebden Bridge? How's life on a boat?"

"Well, you know, can't complain."

He began to sing deep and rasping like Rod Stewart, *"I am sailing, I am sailing…"*

"Dave!" I said irritably.

"Oh, come on, Jenny, where's your sense of humor?"

"Out of the window today, I'm afraid. I've got a hangover!"

"What, on a school day? You were out last night?"

"Yes, I was."

"Well, I…"

"What, Dave? Well, what?"

"Well, who with?"

"A friend."

He gave a dry chuckle, "A man?" And when I didn't reply straight away, burst out with, "Jenny, a man?"

"Yes, a man, Dave. Why? What's the problem?"

He sputtered a bit before saying, "Didn't take you long to replace me, did it?"

"Andy isn't a replacement for you, Dave."

"Oh, Andy, eh?"

A hot rage boiled up inside me, "You've no right to question me, Dave. We split up, remember? You wanted a brand-new life in New York, and I didn't."

"Ah yes, dear Jenny," he said sweetly, cajoling as if I was a five-year-old child, "But I wanted you to come with me."

"Dave, did you hear what I said just now? I didn't want to go. I'm quite happy living here alone on my boat, and from everything you tell me about your new life, you're happy, too, or is it all hot air?"

"Well, well," Dave sputtered, but I carried on, uncaring now, on a red-hot roll.

"So, dear Dave, there's no need to check in with me almost every day. Live your life, Dave, have a good one!"

And I hung up, shaking now, fully riled up, almost throwing my phone at the wall until common sense prevailed and I kept it tightly in my hand where immediately it began to buzz. I glanced at the pulsing screen, the words *"Dave calling"* clearly visible, but I ignored it and let it ring and ring, and then it buzzed. He must have left a voicemail.

He sounded angry and hurt, bewildered even, *"Jenny, you hung up on me. Ring me back. We need to talk about this. Come on now, ring me… please…"* There was a pause and a clicking, and then quietly, *"Please."*

Shaking my head, I went into the tiny kitchen where I dissolved a couple of headache tablets in water and drank them down quickly, leaning against the sink, determined now to leave things as they were with Dave. There was absolutely no need for him to "check in" every day, as he called it. He'd chosen his new life over me, and it was time he drew a line beneath our relationship and moved on.

Feeling quite rejuvenated, a sudden urge to

write came over me, and I hastened into the sitting area, where I pulled the laptop out and brought up my novel *"Hidden Desires"* onto the screen. Now, where did I get to? What had Jeanette and Josh been up to the last time I'd been in their world. I was determined that today was the day where they got together, and the romance began. Conjuring up a picture of the very desirable Andy Valentine to give me inspiration, I began to type, my fingers flying so fast over the keyboard that my thoughts could barely keep up.

"It's as if I've never really seen you before," said Josh, as Jeanette let her hair down so it flowed smooth and silky over her bare shoulders.

"You just haven't been looking," she replied, staring into his eyes, enticing him with her good looks.

Josh gazed at her, reveling in her beauty and wanting her so much. With that thought in mind, he began to move closer, and closer still…

***

My phone beeped, and I picked it up, seeing the little envelope icon indicating that a text message had come through. It was from Emma. *"Hi Mum, here's the contact details for the hypnotist that you were asking about. His name is Woody Linford, and his practice is on 56 Bank Lane, Hebden Bridge, 01422 879121. And his website (worth a look) is woodlin@hypno.co.uk. Let me know if you make an appointment. See you soon x."*

Scribbling down the number, the thought, "Andy wants me to do it," spurring me on, I went ahead and made the call.

CHAPTER SIX

Nineteen-Ninety

"Good night, Jenny, you've been excellent today. Born to work with children, I think."

Red-faced, I said shyly, "Thank you, Miss Lynch, I've enjoyed it too."

"Oh, call me Vanessa," she said airily, "After all, we're going to be working together for the next two weeks," She gave me a dazzling smile, "And I shall definitely look forward to seeing you tomorrow at eight sharp, okay?"

I nodded as Vanessa carried on, "You seemed to bond very well with Susie. She's a lovely little girl, isn't she? So sweet and very confident once you get to know her."

"Yes, she's lovely."

"Have you any brothers and sisters, Jenny? I feel you've had experience with small children?"

Sadly, I shook my head, "No," I hesitated,

wanting to talk about my sister, but afraid. Mum and Dad discouraged it, always silencing me with a dead-eyed stare. Sometimes it felt good though, to speak of her, to say her name, so her life didn't seem like a dream, that she'd been real, that she'd really existed.

She bent at the waist so she was nearer to me, her face close to mine, "Are you okay?"

I took a deep breath, "My sister died, Miss. She was called Maisie, and she wasn't very well, she had Spina Bifida? That's…"

"Yes, I know what it is. Oh, Jenny, I'm so sorry," she looked awkward and embarrassed as I said, "It's okay, Miss, but can I go now, or I'll be late for my appointment."

Miss Lynch let me go then, and I left, the heat hitting me hard like a punch to the stomach as I went out onto the street. The busy street where cars raced by, and the traffic lights changed quickly from red to green and back again, and the pedestrian crossing beeped manically at regular intervals. Two boys on bikes raced past, one of them swerving dangerously on the pavement, almost knocking me over. They made a beeline for a large blue van that was parked at the curb, and I could hear their high, sweet voices shouting at somebody, the driver perhaps, who sat inside, idly thumbing through a newspaper.

"Oy, gypos," said one of them, whilst the other

said, "Nah, my dad calls em bloomin' pikies!" They both laughed uproariously and stopped cycling, their feet on the ground, legs straddling their bikes, whilst one of them threw a stone that hit the passenger side of the blue van, making a dent. Immediately, the driver's door opened, and a man got out. A youngish man sporting a bald head, a brightly colored tattoo of a snake slithering its way up his neck, and another one, a crudely drawn black cross, on his cheek. He wore blue jeans and a tight white tee shirt.

I suddenly felt sick; it must be because it was so warm, and everything around me seemed to fade in and out, the boys disappearing and the man too, the blue van shimmering in the heat until that too faded away to nothing and even the traffic became quiet, muted until all I could hear was my own panicked breathing, rasping in and out, in and out, as if I was fighting for air.

A voice whispered in my ear, *"It's okay, Jenny, stay calm, but don't come back yet. Go back to sleep, go back to nineteen-ninety. You're in the street. There's a blue van and two boys on bikes. They've thrown a stone at the van, and they're shouting at the driver, and he's got out of the van and is walking towards them. Go back, Jenny, go back. Look at the van. Try to get the registration number."*

"You little devils," shouted the man with the tattoos, "You wait until I get hold of you two!" The boys laughed and cycled away, shouting even more derogatory words over their shoulders."

The man stood, his face angry, ugly even, shaking his fist at the rapidly disappearing boys as they cycled away. He inspected the van closely, running his fingers over the dent, where the paint had uncurled, showing the silver beneath. Fumbling in his pocket, he pulled out a battered packet and, putting a cigarette to his lips, lit it with a match and stood, his back against the van, inhaling deeply and pulling at the cigarette with his teeth as smoke spiraled from his nose and his mouth. Suddenly, he caught sight of me staring and, eyes narrowed, threw the glowing stub to the ground and began to walk towards me, slow and stealthy as a panther.

The voice echoed in my head, *"Look at the registration number, Jenny, the registration number of the van."*

Glancing at the van again, the number *198 NCG* wavering in front of my eyes, I turned and walked quickly to the pedestrian crossing, pressing the button with shaking fingers. *198 NCG* as I heard hurried breathing behind me and felt the weight of a hand on my shoulder. *198 NCG* as I glanced around, my eyes wide, my heart clattering like an express train.

"You dropped something," said a lady standing behind me. She wore a yellow summer dress and had a straw basket hooked over her arm. She wore lipstick, the color red and glossy, like a slash of blood across her face, "Here," She thrust something into my hand. I took it from her. A piece of paper? Before I could reply, she chattered on, "Be careful, dear, the traffic's so busy. Don't cross until you see the little green man."

"Yes," I said quietly, "Thank you miss."

The little green man appeared, beep beep beep, and the traffic stopped, so I hurried across the road, glancing behind me expecting to see the bald man standing there, still staring, his arms crossed over his muscular chest, but with a pang, I saw the van had gone, had disappeared as if it had never been there. With a parting smile and a wiggle of the fingers, the lady walked away, her hips swaying beneath the yellow dress.

Curious I looked at what she'd given me, what I held in my hand. I gazed in disbelief and then looked all around, behind me, to both sides. How could it be? I put it safely into my rucksack for the morning and then, afraid I was going to be late for my appointment, hurried away.

***

Present Day - November

"Are you okay, Jenny?" Andy stared at me, a frown marring his handsome face, two tiny lines in the space between his eyebrows, "Here, drink this."

He handed me a steaming mug of hot coffee, which I took from him, our fingers brushing, and sipped gratefully, wrapping my hands around the mug, "Yes, I'm okay now," although was I? I felt strange, disembodied somehow, part of me here and part of me back there, in nineteen-ninety, with the blue van and the strange-looking man who sported a snake tattoo that slid sinuously around his neck.

Oh, sorry forgot to say, we were in *"Classy Coffee"* again, the café we had been in before when Andy had to sit with me because there was no room. Do you remember? No? Of course, you do. After all, it wasn't that long ago! Come on, dig deep. Do you need to be hypnotized? Lol (and that means laugh out loud).

Well, whatever, we were here again, and it was busy, just as it was before. Yeah, I know, it was a very popular place. All the tables were full, and the waitresses rushed about, holding full trays high above their heads, wearing their tight black skirts and long aprons, brightly colored tattoos covering their arms, their legs, and their necks. There's a general hubbub of talking and laughter, and music plays, a sixties song by the Love Affair, *"The sun always shines, down in my rainbow valley…"* The coffee machine hissed and spurted, a cloud of steam forming in the air.

"Young people these days," I said, shaking my

head, "And their obsession with tattoos ..."

Andy raised his eyebrows whilst picking up a chocolate biscuit and taking a bite, "I know, it used to be just Army men really, braving a tat whilst on a drunken night out." He gave a snort of laughter. *"Bird's sweetest song comes from my rainbow valley..."*

I giggled and said, "Yes, my dad had some, and just as you said, a drunken night out from when he did his National Service."

Andy wolfed down the rest of the biscuit, swallowed, and then took a sip of coffee, "Really? Wow. Oh God, I'm starving. I might have to order something more substantial than these biscuits."

"Yeah, me too. I'm peckish. There's one tattoo you know, I remember clearly, a soldier, sweat dripping from his forehead and the wording, *"Malaya Never Again,"* in all pretty muted colors."

Now, why had I said that? I didn't usually talk about my parents, and I would certainly never utter a word about my dad's tattoos and my sister, oh God, my sister. I'd talked about my sister to somebody, although I couldn't remember who, and I never did that. My heart beat hard and fast. Did Andy know? Had Dr. Linford told him the outcome of the session?

"What was it like then?" Andy asked. He looked excited, his eyes shining, even as he picked up the menu and gave it a cursory glance.

"What, you mean, being hypnotized?"

"Yeah. Hmm, I might have Welsh Rarebit."

"Glorified cheese on toast?" I grinned impishly, "But do you know, I think I'll have that too."

He grinned, "Yeah, I'm in the mood for cheese, and then, glancing at his watch, "It's almost teatime, so...Well?" He looked at me, "Was it like going to sleep?"

I shrugged and took a sip of coffee, "Yeah, he lulled me to sleep with the sound of his voice. He said that some people can't be hypnotized, but I was easily."

"Did you have to stare at a watch swinging backwards and forwards?"

"No," I giggled, "He just used the sound of his voice. I felt sleepy as if I'd had an injection, you know, like before you have an operation and you have to count backwards, ten, nine, eight, and then you're gone?

Andy nodded, "Oh yeah, I know what you mean."

"It's like that, you drift off, and then, instead of just waking up as if you've never been asleep at all, you start having really vivid dreams. I felt as if I was there, which I was, I suppose. I was re-living my life, wasn't I?"

He nodded as I said, "The waitress is just there. Look, if you want to order something."

"Ah, yes," he raised a hand, and the waitress came rushing over, "Could I have two Welsh Rarebits, please?"

"Certainly, Sir."

She made a note on her pad, "Any more coffee?"

Andy and I glanced at each other, he arching his brows as I said, "Yeah, another pot would be great." She hurried away, her slim hips swinging in the tight black skirt.

"Right then. Now that's sorted, do you actually remember anything from the session?"

I took another sip of coffee before looking at Andy from beneath my lashes and saying, "Did Dr. Linford tell you anything?"

"No, of course not. Patient confidentiality and all that."

The door pinged open, and a group of people strolled in, laughing and talking in loud American accents. "Wow, isn't this a quaint place?" They all nodded, agreeing, "Yeah, but everything's so small! I mean, look at this place!" We exchanged amused glances as one of the waitresses fluttered around, showing them to a table and taking their order.

"Oh yes, I did. I saw myself saying goodbye to the manager, Vanessa, I had to leave early for an appointment that day, and then I went outside. The first thing I saw was a blue van parked at the curb, registration number 198 NCG. It was a really hot day, too, but it was June, wasn't it? I was sweating, and the road was so busy, there was loads of traffic, and the pedestrian crossing kept beeping."

"Yeah, it was June," Andy replied, "Certainly a day I'll never forget, and boy was it hot." He frowned and narrowed his eyes, "198 NCG?" He stared into space, thinking hard, "That's an eighties number plate."

"There was a man, the driver of the blue van. He had a tattoo, a snake that curled up his neck, and a cross on his cheek. It was badly drawn, the cross, amateurish, you know?" Andy nodded as if to say, "Yeah, go on, go on."

"Oh yes, and there were two boys on bikes. They almost knocked me over as I stepped outside, and they threw a stone at the van and made a dent on the passenger side."

"Why did they throw a stone at the van?"

Shrugging, I said, "I don't know, I…" Andy poured more coffee into his mug and then indicated towards mine. Absentmindedly, I nodded, busily racking my brains, trying to remember everything from today's session.

"What? What were you going to say?"

"I'm not sure, but," and then suddenly it occurred to me, "The boys didn't like the driver, so they threw the stone, they called him a gypo and something else, um."

"Gypo? That's gypsy?"

"Yeah, they said that, but something else as well. Oh, what was it?" I shook my head in annoyance.

"Pikey?"

I gazed at Andy, open-mouthed, "Yes, that's exactly it, Pikey!"

The lady at the next table gave me a strange side-eyed glare. I'd obviously spoken a touch too loud. Andy noticed and leaned in close. He smelt good of soap and some sort of lemony cologne, making my heart race even more, "That word, it's a bit of a derogatory name, but you know that, don't you?"

I nodded, "Yes, I got that from the driver's response to the boys. He got out of the van, not happy at all. He was strange looking, too, skinny, yet muscular. He had a bald head, shaved, not hair naturally lost, and the tattoos made him look rough and dangerous. Do you know what I mean?"

"Yeah, I do." He drained his coffee and put it on the table, "We've got something to go on, Jenny. Thank you for putting yourself through this. It means a lot to me."

The waitress arrived with our order, "Two Welsh Rarebits."

We thanked her as she put the plates on the

table, together with cutlery and napkins, a cruet set. She rushed away, coming back within a few minutes with another pot of coffee. "Enjoy," she said breezily as she hurried away and the door pinged, and yet more people came piling in.

"Um, this is lovely," I said, taking a bite, "I didn't realize I was so hungry."

"Being hypnotized must be hungry work," commented Andy as he, too, took a bite, followed by another swig of coffee.

"I wonder if we could find Vanessa," I said, "Obviously, she'd have been questioned at the time by the police. Do you remember her?"

"Yeah," I do, vaguely," He cut another piece of the Welsh Rarebit and put it in his mouth, chewing thoughtfully, "A lot of what happened at that time is a blur now, and she was older than us, Jenny, maybe in her thirties so she'd be in her sixties now."

"Yeah, but not in her dotage, right? Sixty is still quite young nowadays, isn't it?"

He laughed, "Yeah, it is so, no, she's not in her dotage. We need to think carefully about all this now. Do you think you might need another session?"

"I'm not sure. I just need to think for a few days. See if anything else surfaces from the depths of my mind," We smiled at each other as we finished our meals and pushed the plates away, after which we drained the coffee and reluctantly rose to leave.

"Come on," said Andy, "I'll walk you home."

It was dusky now, the sky a navy blue, speckled with tendrils of cloud. The canal was busy as it always was, with walkers, cyclists, and runners all vying for space, and the strident honking of ducks and geese rang out in the air, swans padded flat-footed on the towpath, like bright white lights shining in the gloom. As my boat came into view, Andy grasped my elbow and pulled me close to his side, snaking his arm around my waist. "Thank you for today, Jenny. You can't imagine what hope this has given me."

"Well, it'll be great if something comes of it. We need to check out the registration number of the blue van."

"Yeah, and maybe find out if there were gypsies in the area at that time. I've never seen any, but that's not to say they don't come here."

"And the man with the tattoos. If he's still around, we shouldn't have too much trouble identifying him, should we?"

Andy shrugged, "Well, don't forget, if he is still around, he'll be an older man now with a wrinkled neck and wrinkled tattoos."

We both laughed and Andy pulled me close into his body, our noses almost touching and his stubbly beard brushing against my cheeks. "Oh Jenny," he whispered, sending chills down my spine, "I hope you don't get fed up with me and my obsession."

"I doubt it," I said softly, "It's becoming my obsession too."

He pulled back a little and gazed into my eyes, "I like that, your obsession, too. You really want to help me, don't you?"

I nodded as he drew me closer and closer still until his mouth, so soft and sweet, met mine, enveloping me in a seductive haze, my heart hammering so hard, he surely must feel it through the thick layers of clothing that lay between us.

"I've longed to do that," he whispered, "I think since the first time I saw you when I was walking the towpath with Ziggy."

"You mean when you rescued Sydney from drowning in the canal?"

"Yes, but that was just an excuse to talk to you."

"Yeah, I liked you too. I watched you from the window as you walked away."

"Really?" He pulled back a little to look at me, his eyes a dark mossy green. His gaze traveled all over my face, taking in everything it seemed, my eyes, my nose, my mouth, "You're so beautiful."

I blushed, a deep red pulsating all over my face, so I leaned closer and whispered in his ear, "Andy Valentine, you're talking too much. Why don't you just kiss me again?"

"I thought you weren't looking for romance."

"Maybe romance is looking for me," I replied softly and then quietly, "For us."

He smiled a long, slow, sexy smile, and without hesitation, his mouth met mine again, and this time, it stayed there for a very long time.

CHAPTER SEVEN

Present Day

"Have you heard from Dave since your, what shall I call it? Little falling out?" asked Emma. I detected the faint hint of a smile in her voice.

I gave a dry laugh, "Well, I've got to admit, there's been a couple of missed calls, but I've ignored them, I'm afraid. Emma gave a delighted chuckle as I said, "He has to move on from our relationship, Emma."

"You're quite right, Mum. Have you seen anything of Andy? He seems like a nice guy."

A hot flush shot through my body at Andy's name, the kisses we'd shared just the evening before running through my head, "Well, yes, he went with me when I saw the hypnotist, and we went to a café afterwards to discuss it. We're sort of working on this together, you know. Anything I remember could help to lead to his daughter or at least give an insight into what happened to her."

"Yeah, of course..."

"You don't sound very convinced, Emma."

"Of course I am, Mum. I need to speak to you properly about what happened at the session. I'll come over with Milly in a day or two, okay?"

"Okay, I'll..." A loud wailing started up in the background, making me smile.

"I've got to go; Lady Milly is calling me."

"I'll make lunch when you come over. Oh, any news on the building work yet?"

"Oh that, no, more complications, I'm afraid," The wailing intensified, "I can't talk about it now, Milly's roaring her head off. For such a little person, she's surprisingly loud! I'll tell you when I see you."

"Okay."

"See you, Mum."

I clicked off my mobile, laughing to myself at the irate crying from baby Milly. It didn't seem so long ago that it was Emma screaming and me running around after her. Oh, what happy memories I had of Emma as a baby, in the good old days, when Frank and I had been so happy. I felt a sudden yearning for the past, and sighing heavily, I pushed those thoughts out of my head and, thinking of the work I had to do, switched on my laptop and, pulling it towards me, brought my novel *"Hidden Desires,"* onto the screen.

Now, where did I get to? Ah yes, *"Jeanette was aware of Josh's eyes roving over her legs as she climbed up onto the bar stool, her skirt riding up to her thighs. She tugged at the hem, pulling it down a little only for him to lean forward and gently touch her hand, "No, don't do that."*

"Do what?" she replied, giving him a coy side-eyed glance.

"Pull your skirt down like that. You've got lovely legs. Why not show them off?"

"What, to everybody? I thought they were only for you."

"Hmm," he smiled, narrowing his eyes, creating the most attractive tiny wrinkles, "Well, now you say that…"

Jeanette giggled and picked up her drink, sipping at the bubbly wine and leaving a thick lipstick mark on the rim…

I sighed heavily and slowly shook my head, wondering how on earth Claudia Raines was such a famous author. I was amazed sometimes that people liked to read this stuff. The thought that perhaps I was becoming disillusioned with my writing came to mind that I was writing what I thought was drivel just to appeal to a market that enjoyed the sexual element of a story more than an actual plot. I had a plot, of course, but with a sinking of my heart, I realized it was rather thin.

Maybe my next book should be different. I could

ditch the *"Hidden Desires"* theme and write a proper love story, a real romance with a great plot where only kisses were allowed and where I only alluded to a bedroom scene and didn't actually write intricate details. I could even use my real name, Jenny Clarke, or perhaps Jennifer Clarke. Or use just my initials, J R Clarke (Jennifer Rosemary, yeah, I know), as per J K Rowling. It would be interesting to see if that book became a bestseller.

Even though I should be working, my mind wandered again to yesterday's session with the hypnotist, and the blue van came to mind. What was the registration number of the van? Ah, yes, 198 NCG. Tapping into Google, I brought up the DVLA website and typed it into the registration number box. *"Vehicle details could not be found"* popped up on the screen, as well as contact details, a telephone number, and an email address if further enquiries were needed regarding the vehicle.

"Hmm," I thought, "It's not surprising, really. It was an old van and was probably scrapped years ago, but it would have been so useful to have owner details, the bald man, for example. That's if he actually was the owner at the time. "Now," I thought with a sigh, "Andy and I would never know."

My phone started to ring, making me jump. Picking it up, I checked it carefully, making sure that there was no "Dave calling" flashing on the screen. I really didn't want to speak to Dave just yet. To my surprise, there was no mention of Dave, only "Andy calling" pulsating with a vengeance. My heart racing, I picked it up and held it to my ear.

"Hello?"

"Hi, Jenny? It's Andy. I hope you don't mind me calling you. I'm…"

"No, of course not. Is there anything wrong? Are you okay?"

"Yes, of course. Are you? Do you still want to see me after last night?"

I laughed a little, "Of course I do. Why wouldn't I?"

"Well, I got quite carried away with your charms. I hope it wasn't too much…" His voice trailed away, and there was a beep on the line that sounded like a text message coming in.

"Too much?" I thought to myself, "As far as I was concerned, there hadn't been enough yet," although I didn't say that, of course, but instead, said sweetly, "Of course, it wasn't," And then after a moment or two stammered, "Oh Andy, I don't know what to say," I blushed again, my face a hot pulsating red, "I'm blushing."

He laughed heartily, "I'm sorry, I shouldn't have asked you that. I don't suppose there's any need for words when it comes to, dare I say it, a budding romance between two people."

My heart rose as I said, "Ah, a budding romance, eh?"

"Yes, perhaps it is."

There was a self-conscious silence before he said, "Look, I've just finished work. I'm going home to get Ziggy because he'll need a walk, and I wondered if you'd like to meet us for fish and chips in the park."

"Fish and chips in the park! Is it warm enough?" I peered anxiously from the window.

"It's glorious for the beginning of November. Blue sky, fluffy clouds, yellow sun. We've got all the right ingredients for a summer day, as long as we wrap up warm. Brrr."

Giggling I said, "In that case, I'd love to meet you, oh, and Ziggy. What time?"

"About half an hour at Gulliver's, you know, the chippy on the square?"

"That's great. Okay, see you then."

"Oh, before you go, Jenny. Just to let you know, I went on to the DVLA website, but I can't find details of the blue van," I imagined him shrugging, "The vehicle's probably been scrapped."

"Oh, I know, I googled it too. I wasn't going to tell you yet. I didn't want you to be disappointed."

He laughed, and if I closed my eyes, I could see

those tiny little wrinkles gathering around his eyes as if by magic. "Well, I can't say I'm not, but let's just say it didn't surprise me. See you soon then?"

"Yes, see you soon."

With a broad smile etched across my face, I ended the call, glancing at my phone as I did so. There was a tiny envelope icon in the corner of the screen, a text message. I clicked on it, *"Hi Jenny, Dave here checking in. Even though you said I didn't need to! Give us a ring, would you? Or even a text would be nice just to let me know how you are. You don't seem to be picking up your calls x."*

For somebody who was deliriously happy in his new situation, he certainly didn't seem to want to let go of our relationship. Quickly, I texted back, *"Hi Dave, all okay here. Busy writing a new book! Hope you're still enjoying your new life x."*

There, short and sweet but friendly. I pressed the send button and put my phone into my bag. Catching sight of my reflection in the mirror over the fireplace, I despaired at the awful sight that met my eyes. I was a fright! Could I be transformed or even partially transformed in, oh my God, only twenty minutes now? I rushed into the bathroom, my heart beating like a drum, frantically looking for my magic wand so I could perform a miracle.

***

"I think I've found Vanessa Lynch," said Andy as we left the fish and chip shop and made our way to the park, carrying our warm, wrapped bundles in a plastic carrier bag. Ziggy strolled along beside us, sniffing at the air with his long nose and trying to hold back slightly to nudge at the carrier bag that Andy had to keep moving out of his way.

My head spun in Andy's direction so quickly I thought I'd caused myself a whiplash, "What? Well, you didn't say anything. Oh my God!"

He looked suitably bemused as he replied, "Well, I've just said something now. I couldn't before when we were in the chippy. It's not really something we want or need other people to hear about."

"No, of course not, but, well, where did you find her?"

"I put her name into Facebook and whoosh, several people came up. I think I've pinpointed her, though, not so much from the photograph but from the fact that she was the manager at *"Toddy Tots Nursery"* back in the day. I need you to have a look at her and see what you think?"

"I'm surprised she's still called Lynch. Most women go by their married name, don't they? Making them really hard to find."

"That probably is her married name, Jenny. Don't forget she was a lot older than us at the time, mid-thirties, you were only sixteen and I was, um, twenty-two. She was either already married then or has never married at all."

"Oh yes, you could be right," I gave him a cheeky grin, "She's had a long marriage then."

"Well, yes, she certainly has."

The park was busy with people strolling along in the unexpected late afternoon sunshine. Children and adults pedaled along on bikes, cutting close in front of runners who puffed and panted in indignation. Children played on the swings and slide, and several spun around and around on the roundabout, shouting out to each other in high, sweet voices, reminding me of the two boys on bikes that I'd seen on that fateful day when little Susie went missing.

Another memory nudged at my mind, something I couldn't quite hold on to, something that kept slipping out of my grasp. Putting it on hold for now, I pointed to a bench by the bowling green, where a group of elderly people were puttering around, dribbling a ball backwards and forwards, "Shall we sit here? My stomach's rumbling. I don't think I can wait much longer for food."

Andy laughed, "Yes, I must say, I'm peckish, too, and the smell of fish and chips is very enticing. Come on, Ziggy, sit down, boy."

We sat down, Ziggy at our feet, gazing at us

expectantly as Andy produced a plastic folding dish into which he deposited Ziggy's portion and placed it in front of him. Before we'd barely started ours, he'd wolfed his down and was sitting back on his hind legs, big brown eyes darting from one of us to the other in great anticipation of yet more food.

"These fish and chips are delicious," I said as I ate another piece of fish followed by a couple of chips, and, unable to resist him, put more in Ziggy's bowl as I did so.

"Yeah, the best in Hebden," Andy glanced at me, "You haven't had them from there before?"

"No."

He grinned, "You haven't lived."

We smiled at each other, and Andy leaned in close and kissed me, his lips warm and salty against mine. My heart clattered uncontrollably in my breast as, Ziggy, an outraged look on his furry face, gave a loud "woof."

"Hey, I still love you, Ziggy boy," said Andy soothingly as he put his last few chips into Ziggy's bowl and, screwing up the fish and chip paper, stood up and put it into a nearby bin. Sitting down again, he took his phone from his pocket and, after a tap here and there, brought up the picture of the person he thought could be Vanessa Lynch. "Look, Jenny, what do you think?"

Peering at the screen, I said, "Yes, I'm pretty sure

that's her. I'd recognize that mass of hair anywhere. It fascinated me when I was a sixteen-year-old kid."

Andy laughed, throwing back his head, showing off the length of his neck and the slice of chest scattered with wiry hairs at the open neck of his shirt. My heart beat hard and fast as he put his arm around my shoulders and pulled me closer, his body warm against mine. Slowly, he shook his head, "You are funny, Jenny."

"My mum and dad always said I had a strange sense of humor."

"Your mum and dad? Yeah, what happened to them, Jenny. They must have been fairly young when they died?"

I stiffened immediately, my heart racing but for a very different reason, "Um, yeah, it was a car accident."

"Oh no," he pulled back slightly and gazed at me intently, "I'm so sorry."

"That's okay, it was a long time ago now, Andy."

"Yes, but…"

"Really, Andy, I don't often talk about them." My mind raced back over the years, especially the years after my sister died, the cold, silent house, and me, a lonely fourteen-year-old girl tiptoeing around the rooms, mum and dad barely speaking to each other, let alone to me. A thick black cloud of depression seemed to hover over me as it always did when delving into the past. At least, the past before I had met Frank and given birth to Emma.

"Hey," Andy took my hand and squeezed it, the gesture warm and comforting and somehow reassuring. Even Ziggy, his warm body leaning against my legs, gazed at me with sympathy in his big brown eyes. Andy glanced at his watch, "I really don't want to go, but I have to take Ziggy home and then back to work for me, I'm afraid, I've got a meeting."

We stood up and began to stroll slowly out of the park, making our way towards the canal, Ziggy walking beside us, stopping every now and then to sniff in amongst the piles of brightly colored leaves that were strewn all over the paths like confetti.

"Oh yes, anything interesting?"

"Oh, the usual thing at this time of year, the light's switch on conflab with the Events Committee."

"Lights?" I frowned at him, "What lights?"

He gazed at me in wonder and began to laugh, "Um, the Christmas lights?"

"Christmas? Oh my God, yes! I'd forgotten about that."

"Forgotten Christmas? Never! Oh, dear me, Jenny," He stopped for a moment, wiping underneath his eyes with a fingertip, "You do make me laugh."

I giggled and shrugged and then, delving into

my coat pocket, handed him a tissue, "Here, wipe your eyes," and when he looked at me, "It is clean."

"Thanks."

"Oh, you know what it's like. Christmas always seems to come around too soon. What happens at this switch on, then?

He dabbed at his eyes before saying, "Well, it's great, you'll have to come along. Santa himself is switching on the lights. Kids love it. We have a band playing, and people run around dressed like elves and fairies. It's marvelous."

"Sounds good. Yes, I'd like to come. When is it?"

"At the end of this month. I'll let you know."

"Okay, talking about Christmas, though, I don't know how I'll manage to cook a decent dinner in my tiny kitchen."

"Come to mine then. I can cook, and I do a mean roast turkey."

I giggled, "Oh Andy, that would be good, but there's Emma, and Jack, her husband, and the baby, of course. They usually come to my place."

He shrugged, "Bring them with you. We'll have a party, with six of us it would be great."

Frowning and counting on my fingers, I said, "Five of us, surely."

"I think you're forgetting Ziggy," he said,

putting on a mock sad face whilst staring at the dog, who gazed back with a mournful expression. "Anyway, think about it. I'd love to cook Christmas dinner for all of you, so, really, it would be my pleasure."

"Okay, well, I'll let you know. I'll speak to Emma."

"Right, well, I've got to be heading home, Jenny. Um, do you fancy doing something at the weekend? Maybe go for a drink? I could text if you like."

"Yes, that would be good," Smiling at me, those wonderful wrinkles fanning out around his eyes, he leaned in close and brushed his lips against mine, and then whispered, "I'll be in touch."

I patted Ziggy and then watched them as they walked away, thinking how much I enjoyed just, well, watching him, Andy, I mean, not Ziggy, lol (laugh out loud), when a sudden thought came to mind, and I called his name, "Andy."

He turned around, his face a white oval in the darkness that had suddenly descended, "Yes."

"Shall I contact Vanessa Lynch?"

"Um, well, do you think it would help?"

"Yes, I do," And when he said yes, I replied, "Okay, I will."

He nodded and waved, his hand a little white flag. I stood there for a moment or two, a stone's throw from my cozy boat, and watched as the street lights came on, lighting up the towpath with an orange glow. Ducks, their heads tucked under iridescent wings, stood motionless at the water's edge as a breeze gently pried colorful leaves from the trees, where they whirled in the air before floating gently on the still brown waters of the canal. Shrugging my shoulders to my ears, it had turned chilly after the warm sunshine earlier. I let myself into my boat and firmly closed the door.

CHAPTER EIGHT

Present Day

"Dave?"

"Hi Jenny," His voice sounded urgent, afraid, "Please, don't hang up."

"What number are you ringing from? It's not yours. *Dave calling* didn't come up on my screen."

"No, I've borrowed a phone because you'd have ignored me if you'd known it was me, and I really need to speak to you."

"Okay, look, what's up, Dave?"

"Well, it's like this, I think I've made a mistake."

"A mistake?" Hearing a terrible commotion outside, I peered from the window at the usual war of the wildfowl, feathers flying through the air, along with great iridescent drops of water, beautiful against the burning leaves of the trees.

"Yes, leaving you, not so much coming here, but I shouldn't have left you."

I sighed heavily, "But you did, Dave, and now you must move on. You're enjoying your new job, aren't you? And you like living in New York?"

"Well, yeah, the job's good and New York is awesome, but I need you, Jenny. I need you here. Come on, broaden your horizons, come out for a visit, see what you think."

My heart beating hard with rage, I answered as calmly as I could, "My horizons are broad enough already, Dave. I like being here in Hebden Bridge …"

"Oh yeah, and with the new bloke, too, eh?"

"Yes, Andy's a nice man, Dave."

"Hmm, Andy, eh! Been on a date, have you?"

"Yes, actually, I've to the pub and a café, and yesterday we had fish and chips in the park."

"The pub, a café, fish and chips in the park?" He erupted into paroxysms of laughter, "Ha, fish and chips in the park, indeed?" And when he'd got over his hilarity, he said with an edge to his voice, "I could wine and dine you in the top restaurants in New York, never mind fish and chips in the park!"

I gripped my phone hard, wishing with all my might it was Dave's neck. I could almost imagine my hands encircling the bulk of it, my fingers pressing in, but I kept a dignified silence, my heart thumping hard, unkind thoughts whirling around in my head, until Dave said, "Jenny, you still there?"

"I'm still here, Dave and, to tell you the honest truth, you're going about this in totally the wrong way."

"Jenny, I…"

"No, Dave, listen. We've split up, okay? I've met someone else. Now, I really think for your peace of mind, you should do the same. Live your life, Dave. I'm going now. I'm going to hang up…"

"You'll regret this, Jenny," he snarled, "You will definitely regret this…"

"What's happened to you, Dave? You're a changed man. What is America doing to you?"

He didn't reply but just snarled again, "I mean it, Jenny, you'll regret this."

I clicked off the call and laid down my phone, my hands shaking. "Coffee," I thought, "Thick black coffee," The only thing that could help me now.

Going into the kitchen, I switched on the kettle that purred to life, as did Sydney, who, trying to crawl up my legs, begged for treats. I gave her biscuits that she wolfed down happily as I made a big mug of coffee, drinking it greedily, feeling the caffeine shoot through my body like fire, giving me strength.

"Right," I thought, pulling my laptop towards me, "Forget about Dave. Think about Andy and his many charms, then inspiration will come." Josh looks like Andy. Describe his stubbly dark beard, his mossy green eyes, and his moist red lips. Oh yes, this was it. I was on a roll.

"Josh grabbed Jeanette, pulling her close towards him, reveling in the feeling of her bare skin against his. Her long, silky hair whispered against him, sending a thrill through his body. She rubbed her cheek against his, "I love your beard," she said seductively, "Your mossy green eyes and your lips red as roses."

"Hmm, now, shouldn't Josh be saying that to Jeanette? Quickly, I deleted the last few lines to read, *"Josh put his hand against her cheek. It felt smooth and silky. "I love your blue eyes," he said seductively, "And your lips, soft as the petals of a rose."*

"Does Jeanette have blue eyes, or are they hazel? Hastily, I scrolled up, frantically reading each line of the manuscript, until I found, *"Jeanette's hazel eyes gazed into his…"*

"Hazel, oh God, not blue at all…"

"I love your hazel eyes," he said seductively, "And your lips, soft as the petals of a rose."

"I love your stockings," she whispered back, "Nobody looks as good as you in stockings."

I took another sip of coffee inhaling its fragrance, its warmth burning my lips, powering me on to write more when I noticed my mistake. "No, Josh isn't wearing stockings, it's Jeanette. Back in the day, I'd have grabbed a red pen and put a bold stroke through it. What absolute rubbish! Pushing the laptop away, I decided to leave it for now, blaming Dave for my inability to get back into the flow, and ring Emma so, picking up my phone, I scrolled through the contacts list and pressed on her name. My phone began to buzz, and then, "Hello?"

"Emma, it's only me, Mum."

"Hi, Mum. I was just about to ring you."

"How's my little granddaughter today?"

"Sleeping at the moment. I'm keeping my fingers crossed she stays that way for a while so I can get some housework done."

"Well, if you need a babysitter, Emma, I can be free. I'm not doing too well with writing at the moment and with all the interruptions from Dave..."

"Dave? So, he's still ringing you?"

"Yes, seems as if he regrets leaving me now, although, in his words, "New York is awesome and his job is great. He even rang me from a different phone today so I wouldn't know it was him."

"Really? He's probably jealous you're seeing that guy, Andy. That's if you told him about him?"

"Oh yes, I've told him. I also told him he should try to meet somebody, too."

"Yes, he should. I don't know who he'd get, though. Ha, he's eaten up with jealousy, totally pea green with it."

I giggled and said, "Well, I wish he wasn't. Oh well, less of Dave. I rang to ask about your building work, Emma. You said there was a problem."

"Oh my God, yeah, the builders can't start yet…"

"Well, isn't that a good thing? After all, you don't want the houses there anyway."

"Well, yeah, I see what you mean, but the reason they can't build is because the gypsies are back…"

"Gypsies?" My ears pricked up as if they were radars.

"Yes, we've had them here before. They lived on the field for months because the farmer just couldn't get rid of them, and when he finally did, they'd left a total mess. It's up to the builders now, though. It's their field, so their responsibility to make them go."

"I didn't know you had gypsies?"

"Yes, only once since we moved in the house, but apparently, they've been coming here for years."

"Can you see them now?" I asked urgently.

"Well, yes, some of them, milling around. I can also see caravans, camper vans, lines of washing, and kids running around. You get the picture?"

"Is there a blue van?" I didn't really know why I asked her that. I knew I was grasping at straws. After all the van had probably been scrapped long ago if it wasn't showing up on the DVLA website.

"I can't see a blue van from here, but that doesn't mean there isn't one. I could go outside later and take a look and ring you back."

"Yes, okay, if you don't mind."

"No, of course not, but what's it all about mum? What's with the blue van?"

"It's something I saw when I was hypnotized, and, well, it's a long story, Emma. I'll tell you all about it when I see you."

"Okay, oh no," I heard a wailing from up above. Lady Milly has surfaced."

I laughed as I hung up, shaking my head at Emma calling Milly "Lady Milly." I picked up my mug and took a sip of coffee, which was stone cold now and tasted so awful that I almost spat it into my beautiful glossy cheese plant that sat like a great triffid on the floor beside the TV. It's far too big for this little boat, really, but I couldn't bear to let it go. A beep sounded from the laptop, indicating that an email had come through.

"Ah," I thought, gazing at the screen, "It's from the hypnotist, Woody Linford."

"Dear Mrs. Clarke

Thank you so much for attending a Hypnotherapy Session with me on Tuesday. I hope it's helped somewhat in your endeavors to unravel the past. I attach a transcript of your thoughts that surfaced during the session which I hope you will find interesting.

Please do not hesitate to contact me again if you wish to discuss the transcript or feel you would like another session.

Best wishes.

Woody Linford (C.Ht)

Clicking on the attachment, I brought up the transcript and read it through, my eyes quickly scanning the pages. A paragraph caught my eye, *"You dropped something," said a lady standing behind me. She wore a yellow summer dress and had a straw basket hooked over her arm. She wore lipstick, the color red and glossy, like a slash of blood across her face, "Here," She thrust something into my hand. I took it from her. A piece of paper? Before I could reply, she chattered on, "Be careful, dear, the traffic's so busy. Don't cross until you see the little green man."*

"What had she given me?" I remembered the lady now because she was pretty and wore a lovely summer dress, but the most important thing was that a grown-up talking to me was amazing. Not many did, only teachers and Vanessa Lynch and now this lady. I'd lived for the past two years with my parents in a silence so palpable that it was like living behind a thick stone wall, cut off from everybody. I'd learned to be quiet, to not speak if I could help it, because nobody answered anyway. Even so, the nagging thought, *what had she given me?* echoed around my head. I had no memory of carrying anything except for my rucksack when I left the nursery that day.

My phone beeped, and a text message popped up, taking my thoughts away from the mysterious piece of paper I'd dropped so many years ago. It was from Andy, *"Hi Jenny, did you manage to contact Vanessa Lynch? Any news you've got would be good. Fancy going out on Saturday night? X"*

Immediately, I clicked out of emails and typed *"Facebook"* into Google and then into the search bar, *"Vanessa Lynch."* Andy was right, a lot of Vanessa Lynch's popped up, but I saw *our* Vanessa straight away, recognizing her immediately because of her great mop of hair. I clicked onto her page to see pictures of her and a man, who I assumed to be her husband, on holiday, soaking up the sun in Italy, Spain, Crete, and other far-flung places, pictures of them at weddings and parties and Vanessa out with groups of girlfriends, on hen nights and weekends away.

There were even pictures of the food she'd eaten or cooked or that her husband had cooked, almost a whole page of culinary delights. She certainly seemed to enjoy a full life. No pictures of children, though. It didn't look as if she had any. I clicked on send a message, *"Hello Vanessa, I don't know if you remember me, but my name is Jenny Clarke. I did work experience with you many moons ago at "Toddy Tots Day Nursery."*

Now, should I mention Susie Valentine, or would it put her off seeing me? I had to give a reason for contacting her, though, didn't I? After all, it wasn't as if we'd been friends and needed a catch-up or that we'd been fellow teachers. I'd been a sixteen-year-old girl, as green as grass, going through a bad time in her life while she was an experienced teacher/manager, happily married by the sound of it, with all the world at her feet.

"I wonder if we might meet. I'd like to talk to you about Susie Valentine. Please let me know if that would be possible. My email address is Jennyc@hotmail.com.

It would be good to hear from you.

"There," I thought as I pressed the send button, "I'd just have to wait now. Hopefully, she'd reply. Picking up my phone, I texted Andy, *"Hi Andy, yes I've sent her a message. Just hope she gets back. Saturday night would be great. X"*

***

Josh confronted Jeanette. He stood bare-chested, the jeans he wore slung low on his hips, his feet bare beneath the flared bottoms. Jeanette moved closer, her hands roving his upper body, his muscles rippling beneath her palms.

"I've something to tell you, Jeanette," Josh said huskily. He clasped her upper arms, pushing her back slightly from his body, but she burrowed into him, planting small urgent kisses on his neck, her lipstick, a deep dark red,

coloring his skin.

"What?" She gave him a coy glance and then burrowed again into his neck, kissing it, tiny little pecks.

"I'm leaving you, Jeanette."

Her head snapped up, her gaze shocked, "You're leaving me?"

"Yes, I have no choice, I..."

"Is there somebody else?"

There was a long silence, a silence that was taut, stretched, impossible it seemed to break until Josh said, "Yes, there is."

Sobs rose up into Jeanette's throat, "Who? Who is she?"

There was another long, taut silence before Josh growled, "It's not a woman. It's a man, Henry." Jeanette looked askance, her pretty face dissolving into salty tears.

Giggling to myself I grew excited at this brilliant twist to the story. After all, my publisher had urged me to take this route many times. I'd always resisted it because of my fan base, I suppose. People tended to rely on the same sort of story from their favorite author, but now, well, maybe now was the time. My fingers flew over the keyboard.

"But you must have known," said Jeanette, "Why didn't you tell me before?"

"Before what?" asked Josh.

"Before I fell in love with you?"

"I didn't know," said Josh softly, "I'm sorry, Jeanette, believe me when I say this isn't what I wanted to happen."

Jeanette reached out to him, but her hands grabbed air as Josh took a couple of steps back, "What happens now?" she asked him tearfully.

Sitting back in my seat and stretching, raising my arms above my head, I thought, yes, what does happen now? What was in the future for Jeanette and Josh? And Henry now, too? A little thinking time was needed, a little break. All I needed on this little break was a glass and a nice bottle of red, maybe even a chocolate biscuit or two, so I could gorge myself while I thought. Oh yes, I was on a high-speed roll and needed to be fuelled. Look out, here I come.

CHAPTER NINE

Present Day

"Did you know that gypsies have set up camp in the field behind Brush Row? Or should I say Bush Row, as the mayor said?"

"Oh yes, that was funny. And Farmer Giles as well. What a hoot, eh? He can be quite vague, can our mayor."

I laughed, "You're telling me. Thank God for the Clerk, eh?" as Andy handed me a glass of wine and, picking up his pint took a long draft. We were at the bar in the Railway pub. The pub was busy, music booming from the jukebox so we had to shout to be heard, and people three deep at the bar.

"Um, yes, but the Clerk can be a bit cantankerous," He gave me a knowing wink, "Anyway, in answer to your question, yes, the builder rang. Very het up. I bet the farmer's glad he sold. He used to have terrible trouble getting them off his land, and I'm sure the builders will, too." He sighed, "This is just another added problem for them. It isn't the best time of year to build anyway, so it could be spring before they make any headway. Oh, look, there's a couple of seats over there. Do you want to sit down?"

I nodded yes as we made our way over to the table. People moved up as we squeezed into the seats, and several people glanced over and raised their glasses. Andy introduced me, "Oh, this is Jenny, Jenny Clarke, a friend of mine. Jenny, this is Jeff. Over there, Pete and Simon. This is Marjorie and Claire."

I nodded to everybody and said, "Pleased to meet you all."

"Oh, by the way, Jeff's in a band, a very good band, actually."

Jeff was a tall, skinny man, impeccably dressed in a smart pale blue suit teamed with a crazy patterned shirt and tie, sporting a trilby with a dashing feather in the brim.

"Oh, really. I do like a good live band."

"Yeah, we're playing at the Trades just before Christmas," He glanced at Andy, "You'll have to bring Jenny along, Andy."

"The Trades Club? Isn't that where Heaven 17 played a couple of years ago?"

"Oh yes, they only have the best bands playing there, you know," Jeff replied with a grin.

"What's your band called?" I asked him.

"The Outta Sights," he said proudly, "We've been playing together for years. Grown old together we have."

"A bit like a family then? What sort of music do you play?"

"Ska mainly, Reggae, you know."

"You mean like Madness and the Specials? That sort of thing." I shrugged, "Or Bob Marley?"

"Well, yeah, similar stuff. Know your music, don't you? Do you like ska then?"

"Oh yes, I love Madness and Bob Marley, of course."

"Well, you'll have to come and see us play then," he replied, "We might be right up your street."

Andy squeezed my hand as Jeff got up and went to the bar, and the others started talking casually amongst themselves. Andy turned to me and smiled, "Well, how's your day been?"

"Oh, fine, very busy writing, I'm on a bit of a roll."

"Ah, so your creative juices have returned, eh? Your sense of romance?" He rolled his eyes.

"Yes," I said, giving him a nudge with my elbow, "Since you came along."

We gazed dreamily at each other, "Actually," I said, "I've added something different. A bit of a twist."

He arched his eyebrows, "Oh, I don't suppose you can divulge?"

I shook my head, "No, sorry, I don't usually discuss my books. I feel it's bad luck."

He grinned, "Okay, I understand that, but I want to have a read when it's published, okay?" I nodded as he squeezed my hand again and moved closer, his thigh very close to mine, sending shivers running down my spine, which I did my best to ignore, as I said, "Can we get back on track now?"

"Of course, actually, I didn't know we were off it." He smiled, his face all wrinkles and dimples, making my heart beat faster.

"It's just that the reason I mentioned the gypsies wasn't because of the hold up to the building work but because of the gypsies themselves."

"What do you mean?" Some of the people surrounding us got up to leave with much hand shaking and goodbyes. The jukebox whirred and clicked, and Donny Osmond began to sing *"Puppy Love."* Andy grinned at me and raised his eyebrows as a group of big men with shaved heads and tattoos began to sing along, swaying to the music and raising their pints in the air as they did so.

I smiled and slowly shook my head, and then said, "The man with the blue van was obviously a gypsy. The little boys shouted at him using derogatory names, definitely not PC now, didn't they?"

"Oh yes, I see what you mean, but it can't be the same gypsies if that's what you're getting at. I don't see what bearing it has on what happened to Susie so long ago."

"But it might be the same ones. Apparently, they return to the same places year after year." I shrugged, "They're families, you see. The man with the blue van might still be with them."

"No, we already found out that the blue van has probably been scrapped."

"Not the man, though. The man won't have been scrapped, will he?"

Andy laughed gleefully, "No, I'm sure he won't have been scrapped, but he might have died."

I shrugged, "Yes, true, he might have died, but he looked to be only in his twenties in nineteen ninety, so he might possibly be in his sixties now."

Andy nodded, "Yeah, you could be right. I suppose it's worth looking into."

"I've already asked Emma to let me know if she sees a blue van or a man with a bald head and tattoos. If not, I'm thinking that maybe we should pay Emma a visit and have a look for ourselves. What do you think?"

"Yes, I think we should. I've met your daughter, but I'd love to see the baby and meet your son-in-law, of course."

The man, Jeff, shouted over to us, "We're moving on now. Nice to have met you, Jenny."

We raised our hands as he moved towards the door, where he stopped and, doffing his hat, said, "I hope to see you both at the Trades Club."

"Love to," we shouted back as they disappeared out of the door, and then turning back to Andy, "Your friends are nice."

"Yeah," he nodded, "I've known them for years now. Ever since I came to Hebden."

"So, you moved to Hebden after Susie went missing?"

He nodded. "Yes, as I told you, my wife and I split up. We're divorced now; she stayed in Tod, and I came here. I had to get away from that place."

"Is she still there, in Todmorden?"

"Yes," His mouth twisted wryly, "Well, I think so. She married again. I don't know if there's any children."

"What's her name?"

"My ex? Fran, Francesca."

Sipping morosely from his pint, he smiled at me, "Shall we change the subject?"

"Okay, I'm sorry." I took a deep breath, "I know I'm rabbiting on about the gypsies, but can the police become involved with evicting them from somebody's land?"

"Oh, yes, but only if a crime has been committed. It's the responsibility of the landowner, you see, a civil matter, and once the landowner gets a court order, they usually move on without a fuss. The police will only intervene under certain circumstances which are set out in the Criminal Justice and Public Order Act 1994."

I took a sip of wine, "Wow, good on you for remembering all the legislation."

He smiled and gave a little dip of his head, saying, "It's my job."

"But what circumstances?" I asked him.

"Well," Andy took a long pull at his beer, "If they believe two or more people are trespassing or preparing to stay for a long period of time, or there's damage to the land or abusive behavior, or if there are six or more caravans or camper vans on the site."

"Oh, well, it seems to me that the police could intervene in this case. I think a visit to Emma is a must."

"Yes, maybe so, but, as I said, they may go quietly for the landowner, the builder. Look, Jenny, I really appreciate you helping me like this for going to the hypnotist," Slowly, he shook his head.

"What are you getting at?"

"I know you saw the blue van and the man with the tattoos as part of your dredged-up memories, I suppose you'd call them, but it doesn't mean that it has anything to do with Susie's disappearance. By the time Susie came out of nursery that day, he and his van may have gone. We could be barking up the wrong tree. That's all I'm saying."

I drained my wine, feeling it travel rapidly down my throat and into my stomach, quietening down the butterflies of anxiety that were fluttering around in there, "Oh God, Andy, I know that. I told you before I went to the hypnotist that it was a hunch, something that was on my mind, something I couldn't explain. I haven't an answer to it, to any of it, but it's worth exploring. You must think it's worth looking into."

I gazed at him imploringly as, leaning in close to me, he grasped my hand, "Of course it is, but it's me, I suppose, and the time that's passed since it happened, I just can't imagine Susie just being there, being somewhere, an adult, a grown-up, maybe with a husband, children," He shook his head helplessly, "I just can't imagine it."

"Have you always thought the worst?"

He gazed at me, his eyes big and deep, fathomless as pools, "Yes, as the years went by."

"Well," I said, "We can only try with this." There was a whirr and a click from the jukebox, and Elton John started to sing *"Your Song"* just as the door opened and a group of people came in, making a beeline for the bar and bringing in a stream of cool night air.

He nodded and said, "Yes, you're right," There was a short silence before he raised his pint and said, "Another drink?"

We had another drink and then made our way back along the canal, enjoying the walk in the cool, clear night, the sky arching above as a great black cavern studded with tiny stars. A tiny breeze shook the trees, shedding the last of the leaves that twirled quickly through the air, softly brushing against our faces as we approached my boat. We stopped outside, and Andy leaned in close and kissed my cheek and then whispered into my ear, "You've no idea how happy I've been since you came into my life, Jenny."

I leaned back a little so I could see his face, "Really?"

"Yes," he nodded as he stared into my eyes, "I'm still on a quest to try and find Susie, but it's not my whole life. I've got somebody else to think about now."

"I know what you mean," I said, "I'd been feeling a bit down until I met you."

"You had?"

I nodded, "Yes, over a long period of time, though, the loss of my husband and then Dave left, and to cap it all, I found myself living on a boat. I, well,

I questioned my state of mind sometimes, but since you came along…" The words trailed away as Andy pulled me in close to his body and kissed the soft skin near my mouth.

I smiled at him and said, "Would you like to come in for coffee, or" I shrugged, "A glass of wine?"

"That would be lovely."

Andy's hand felt warm against mine as we made our way up onto the deck of the boat. Fumbling in my bag, a little light-headed from the wine I'd drunk, I found the key and inserted it into the lock, carefully opening the door. We stepped inside, Andy immediately enclosing me tightly in his arms. His lips sought mine, they tasted of the beer he'd drunk earlier and he smelt spicy, the cologne he wore warm on his skin.

"You're lovely, Jenny, really lovely," he whispered, his breath ragged.

"So are you," I whispered as, not wanting to let him go, I stuck out a foot and, with a little careful maneuvering, carefully closed the door.

***

Hi Jenny, what a surprise to hear from you after all these years. I'm sorry I've been so long in getting back to you, but I've been on holiday with my husband, to Crete, again lol. I do love that place so much. Anyway, yes, I do remember you. Young Jenny Clarke, who was such a great help to me in Toddy Tots Day Nursery for a two-week work experience.

I remember you being so good with children that I thought you should work with them, but, unfortunately, you happened to be there when the lovely little Susie Valentine disappeared. What an awful time that was. I get shivers down my spine every time I think of it. And that's often. Despite how long ago it was. I really hope that incident didn't put you off from pursuing work in that field.

I'd be very happy to meet to talk about Susie, but I really don't know what I could tell you. Everything was investigated by the police at the time, and there was simply no trace of her. Obviously, her parents were distraught. I've often wondered how they are and what happened to them, but as so many years have gone by, I'll probably never know.

Will you please suggest somewhere we could meet? I still live in Todmorden and I've no idea where you live now, so do let me know. I shall look forward to hearing from you, Jenny. Vanessa x

It was raining hard, the pattering on the roof loud in here, inside my little boat, loud as bullets, as if I was under siege, but strangely wild and exhilarating. This was the first time it had rained so hard since I'd moved in. Peering from the window, I could see it coming down in long silver sheets like needles piercing the ground and great round drops that hit the water, churning it up, and all the ducks and geese and even the swans bobbing about as if they were enjoying themselves immensely.

"Hmm," I thought, as I sipped my coffee, my novel *"Hidden Desires"* on the screen of the laptop in front of me, "Fabulous, she wants to meet."

I'd gone on to Facebook, in a sudden blank lull from writing, not sure which way the story was going now, expecting to be disappointed yet again, but a message was there from Vanessa with a clear invitation to meet. Maybe Todmorden should be the place. I used to go to a lovely little café on the Main Street that had really good coffee and excellent homemade cakes and biscuits, and their lemon meringue pie was to die for.

My tummy rumbled alarmingly and, glancing at the clock, realized it was time for lunch, and Sydney too, who had woken up, a furry ball, bleary-eyed and stretching, but, before that, I really should let Andy know about Vanessa.

Picking up my phone, I tapped out a quick message, *"Hi Andy, Vanessa has been in touch and said she'd like to meet. She lives in Todmorden, so I'm going to suggest meeting there in a café on the Main Street called "Love Coffee." I don't know if you've ever been in there, but it's a really nice place. Hope that's okay with you? Let me know, and I'll arrange a date and time x."*

As I pressed the message send button, thoughts of Andy rushed through my mind, and I closed my eyes, bringing up his image in front of me, his handsome face, with its sprinkling of stubble around his cheeks and chin, his eyes, bottomless green pools and his lips red and ripe for kissing. My phone beeped and, so sure it was a message from Andy, I clicked on it straight away. My heart sank as I saw it was from Dave again. Since our argument a few weeks ago, he'd taken to texting most days, saying he was just checking in. This was no different. *"Hi Jenny, just checking in to see how you are. It would be nice if you'd let me know x."*

Afraid that he'd ring, angry and abusive, as he had before, I replied straight away, *"All okay here, Dave."* Yeah, okay, short and sweet, but it should keep him quiet for a day or two.

Stretching and glancing at the screen of the laptop where I was desperately trying to deal with the relationship between Josh and Henry now, as Jeanette had finally got the message and made her weeping way to the train station with a bulging suitcase, leaving the story wide open. I stood up and, stomach rumbling very alarmingly, made my way to the kitchen, closely followed by a meowing Sydney, to find something nice for lunch.

CHAPTER TEN

Nineteen-Ninety and Present Day

I felt a hand on my shoulder, hot and heavy, burning through my tee shirt and onto my skin. I turned quickly, my heart banging like a drum, afraid it was the man with the tattoos, afraid that the man with the tattoos was standing behind me, and it was his hand so heavy on my shoulder. But it wasn't him. It was a lady, a pretty lady wearing a yellow summer dress and a wide-brimmed straw hat, lipstick a slash of red across her face.

"You dropped something," she told me, "Here you are." She held out a piece of paper.

"No," I said, shaking my head and trying to turn away to look back at the road where traffic flowed thick and fast, eager to be on my way. I was afraid of being late for my appointment, "Sorry, but it isn't mine."

"It is," she said, "I saw you drop it. You'd better take it. It might be important. Is it your homework?"

I shook my head but, frowning, took the paper from

her, taking a quick glance as I stepped forward. "Careful dear," said the lady, putting her arm out in front of me, "Don't cross until you see the little green man."

"I won't," I told her.

She smiled just as the green man beeped, and everybody flowed across the road, cars on either side waiting impatiently, their engines revving, drivers, white-knuckled, holding onto the wheel, frustrated because of the delay and the heat. The lady wearing the yellow dress wiggled her fingers at me and walked on, her hips swaying beneath the yellow dress.

Curiously, I looked at the piece of paper again, turning it over and over in my hands, and realizing it was a card, a stick figure of a man, his eyes colored in very green on the front. Smiling, I put it inside my rucksack when suddenly, nausea overcame me, rising up higher and higher in my throat until I thought I would be sick. Everything around me went hazy as if the sun had passed behind a cloud, and then everything began to turn around and around, all in a green and blue blur, as if the world was spinning on its axis, and my heart raced, and I began to pant as if I was a dog running in the heat.

I heard a voice, a calm voice, "It's okay, Jenny, it's okay, let yourself come back. Come back to the present time. Leave nineteen-ninety behind."

My eyes snapped open to come face to face with the hypnotist, Woody Linford. He smiled, his brown eyes twinkling despite the concern in them, "Are you okay, Jenny? Just lie still for a while. You may feel nauseous. Sometimes patients say they feel as if they're spinning before they come back."

"Yes, I do, just a little," I told him.

"Did you find what you were looking for?"

"Yes, I think so," I saw the piece of paper in my hand, the stick man with the very green eyes. Slowly, I nodded, "I must have it somewhere, but I don't remember where I've put it. I don't think I'll have thrown it away."

"What do you mean?"

"I'm not sure. Something I had in my hand, a piece of paper, I mean, a card. It didn't belong to me but to the little girl, Susie." I gazed at Woody Linford.

"Did you take it from her that day?"

"Oh no, no, of course not. I helped her make it. It was for her daddy, a Father's Day card."

"Oh," He looked sad, his face a mass of lines and wrinkles, "Do you think you still have it? At home somewhere?"

"I don't know," I shook my head, tiny little shakes, "I've never seen it. Never once throughout the years. It's strange, don't you think?"

He nodded, "Yes, it is. Poignant somehow, sad," and then, "Do you feel better now? You have some color in your face. You were as white as a ghost."

I laughed and said, "I feel much better now." Shakily, my legs like jelly, I slowly stood up and held out my hand, "Thank you."

He clasped my hand, his grip firm, "Are you sure you're ready to go?"

"Yes."

"If you need me again, you know where I am."

I nodded as I shrugged on my coat, pulled on my hat and a pair of gloves, and made my way out into the cold, dark November night.

***

"It must be somewhere," I thought to myself, "I was holding it in my hand, and I don't remember giving it to Vanessa the following day at the nursery." A hot wave of despair washed over me at the thought that I may have thrown it away. "But I wouldn't have done that, not knowingly anyway."

I racked my brains trying to think of where it could be, and with everything having been packed for moving only a few months ago, the chances of finding it were very remote. I sat on the settee, my head in my hands, the pattering of raindrops still sounding on the roof. Would it never stop? And thoughts rushing through my head. I remembered it as if it were yesterday, Susie drawing on the card, the stick figure that was her daddy, with long limbs and brightly colored green eyes, her little tongue poking out from between her lips as she concentrated.

"Ah," I thought, "I have a box somewhere where I keep all my important papers. Things like birth certificates, marriage certificate, Frank's death certificate, and NHS card. Now, where is it?" Quickly, I delved into the storage space beneath the seats in the sitting area, and, yes, there it was, an old tin decorated with flowers, probably filled with chocolates or biscuits at some point in time.

I searched through, flipping through the documents but there was no card. There were plenty of other cards, cards from milestone birthdays, Emma's 1st birthday and wedding day cards, sympathy cards, that I lingered over for a second or two, but just not that particular one. Discouraged, I put the tin back where I'd found it and stood stock still, aimlessly looking around.

"Coffee," I thought as I went into the kitchen and, switching on the kettle, I nibbled on a biscuit as it came to a boil, my mind racing over the possible places where the card could be, only to come up with a total blank. Sydney appeared, winding in and out of my legs, so I fed her treats that she ate, crouching and purring over her bowl.

Taking the coffee into the living area, I peered from the window. The rain had eased now (thank goodness, the constant drumming on the roof was driving me mad, as well as the ever-present urge to use the loo, what was it about running water?), and a watery sun shone in a pale blue washed-out sky. A breeze pried brightly colored leaves from the branches of the trees, scattering them over the ground and the murky water of the canal.

I shivered, hunching my shoulders to my ears and, fetching a blanket, draped it around my shoulders, knowing that I'd need to fetch more coal if I wanted to light the wood burner. It could be hard work living on a boat. Sighing, I sat down and looked again at the screen of the laptop as Sydney climbed up onto my lap and settled herself, a warm, pulsating ball of fur.

"Has she gone, Josh?" asked Henry.

"Yes, she left last night," Josh replied, "So we can be together now. There's nothing to keep us apart."

Henry smiled, his eyes widening, "So I won, huh?"

Josh frowned, "There's no winner or loser, Henry. It's not like that. It's the fact that I love you, not Jeanette." He took a step forward, noticing Henry's physique, the bulging muscles on his arms, his square jaw and dark eyes, the sprinkling of black stubble on his cheeks and his chin…

"Oh no, was Henry beginning to look like Andy? I was using him as inspiration far too much. Hmm, maybe a change of Henry's look was necessary.

Unable to concentrate, Josh and Henry taking a back seat for now, I took several deep breaths and slumped into the cushions of the settee, idly stroking Sydney, feeling her little body rise and fall with her breathing, thinking and thinking about the card, in fact, I was thinking so hard, my head was beginning to ache. "Why did I have the card anyway? It wasn't even mine. Regardless of what had happened to Susie, she should have had it with her when she left the nursery that day, so how did it come to be on the ground when I went outside?"

A sudden terrible feeling shot through my body, "Had Susie followed me outside, giving the man with the tattoos a chance to take her and spirit her away in the blue van?" I took several panicked breaths, trying to think straight, trying to sort things logically in my mind. I closed my eyes and saw myself again, taking the card from the lady wearing the yellow dress. What did I do with it then?"

Closing my eyes, I tried to transport myself back to nineteen-ninety, willing myself back, and then I knew, I could see myself doing it, "I put the card into my rucksack," the little rucksack that I'd been so proud of, a big step up from a satchel and so much easier to carry than a briefcase, and at the same time, my heart sank, right down into my fluffy slippers at the thought that my rucksack will have been long gone. I don't remember seeing it over the years and why would I keep it anyway? Oh, how I'd longed to show Andy his daughter's card the next time I saw him, an impossible dream, or so it seemed at the moment.

My phone beeped, and picking it up, I saw it was a text message from Dave, *"Hi Jenny, how's things? Hope all good. Ring when you get the chance x."*

Despite his threats last time we'd spoken, his snarled words, *"You'll regret this, Jenny,"* it seemed he just couldn't leave me alone. An irritational rage welled up inside me, and the thought, "Dave's becoming my stalker," flashed through my mind. I was just about to ring him and give him a piece of my mind when the phone rang, *"Emma calling,"* flashing on the screen.

"Hi, Emma?"

"Mum, how are you? Just thought I'd check in," She giggled, "A gentle Dave reminder!"

"Oh, Emma, talking of Dave. He's just texted me again, asking me to ring when I get a chance. Do you think this is stalker behavior?"

"Yes, it is. You should ring him and tell him to back off or get the police onto him."

I laughed, "I was just about to when you rang, and, no, I don't really want to involve the police. I've got something more pressing to worry about."

"What? What's more pressing than having a stalker?" I imagined Emma standing there, one hand on her hip, the other pressing her phone to her ear, a look of amazement on her pretty face.

"It's something that cropped up when I was hypnotized, a memory, and I really wish I still had my old school rucksack."

"I've got your rucksack, Mum. Oh, hang on a minute, Lady Milly's whimpering, I'll go and get her. Hold on, Mum."

"She's got my rucksack," I thought, "Emma's got my rucksack, but how? When?" My heart beating fast. I held my phone close to my ear as Emma put hers down. I could hear music playing in the distance, maybe from the radio, an old song from the '60s, *"Tired of waiting, tired of waiting for you ..."* and then, "I'm back, Mum, I think Milly's hungry, so I can't be too long."

"Okay, but did I hear you right? You've got my rucksack?"

"Yeah, don't you remember? You gave it to me ages ago, asked me to take care of it, and you said my first child could have it when they're older."

"Oh my God, I can't believe it. I thought I'd lost it years ago."

"No, it's here somewhere. I'll have to search, but it's definitely here. Why do you want it so urgently?"

"Have you ever looked in it?"

"No," A loud wailing suddenly sounded into my ear so I had to pull my phone away.

"Oh my God, is Milly's voice getting louder, or

is it just me?"

Emma laughed, "I know, it's shrill, really shrill. What did you say about the rucksack."

"Just that I'm hoping what I'm looking for is inside it. It's a card. I'll explain later. I could call round, or maybe you could have a look inside and let me know if you find anything."

"Okay, once I get Milly down, I'll search for it. I'd better go. She's acting as if she's starving. See you, Mum."

I hung up then, shaking my head, wondering how I could have forgotten that I'd given Emma the rucksack. Was I becoming forgetful at not even fifty years old? Or was it the stress of the past few years, all the upsets I'd dealt with, first of all, Frank dying and then Dave going and then selling the house, buying the boat? And now my relationship with Andy and the search for his missing daughter?"

My phone buzzed, the screen coming alive, the words *"Dave calling"* pulsing. "Right," I thought, "Unfortunately for Dave, he'd caught me at a bad time. I was going to have to make it clear to him that his behavior was becoming irrational, and there was no doubt he was behaving like a stalker."

I picked up the phone and took several deep breaths to calm myself before I spoke.

***

"Hi Andy, I've made a date to meet with Vanessa. Saturday at 2.00pm in the café "Love Coffee," in Todmorden. You said you'd been in years ago and liked it. I mentioned I'd be bringing somebody with me. She said it was fine. She didn't ask who, so I didn't tell her. There'll be time enough for explanations when we see her. I hope you're okay. Text back or ring if you fancy a chat. Hopefully, see you Saturday x

***

"Mum?"

"Hi, Emma. Is my little granddaughter settled now?"

"Oh yeah, she downed her bottle in one. She was that hungry."

We giggled, after which there was a short silence until I said, "Emma?"

"Mum, I found the rucksack."

"You did, oh my God. Well?"

"It's empty, Mum."

"Empty?"

"Yeah, not a thing inside. I've searched and searched, and, well, it's definitely empty."

Once again, my heart plummeted right down into my fluffy slippers, and a feeling of disappointment surged through my body. "Okay, thanks, Emma … thanks for looking for it."

"Look, Mum, I know you're disappointed, but, well, maybe it was a false memory, and you didn't pick it up at all, or maybe the card just went missing over the years. It's been a long time, hasn't it?"

"Yes, you're right. It's been a long time."

"I'll be in touch, Mum."

"Okay, Emma, see you soon."

I clicked off the call and sat back into the cushions, defeated. I'd been so sure the card was in the rucksack. So very sure. My phone beeped. A text message from Andy. *"Hi Jenny, what are you doing now? Could I call round for a chat? I'm longing to know about the session with the hypnotist. I'll bring a bottle of red x."*

Smiling at the phone, my heart lifting for the first time that day, I clicked on reply, *"Yes, of course you can. A bottle of red would be great. See you soon x."* I even finished the message with a little smiling emoji just to let him know how happy I was.

I bustled around then, tidying up, dragging in from the deck a bag of coal, and piling several chunks into the wood burner. I inhaled the smell of sulfur as I lit a match and watched until the fire took and spread, soon burning a warm red glow. I set out two glasses on the table and put crisps and peanuts in bowls. I had pizza if he fancied some later. Finally, I glanced in the mirror and tidied my hair, replenished my lipstick, and checked that I looked okay wearing jeans and a long-sleeved tee shirt, a picture of Marc Bolan wearing his top hat as *"The Slider"* on the front.

I pouted this way and that, wondering if I looked as good as a supermodel, but no, I was no Kate Moss or Naomi Campbell, and not a Twiggy either, even at her age! It was just me and, do you know what, that would just have to do. I heard a tap on the door and, my heart racing, I shouted out, "Come in," and stood waiting until, smiling, his face all cute dimples, Andy walked towards me, and I opened my arms wide for him.

CHAPTER ELEVEN

Present Day

Andy nudged me and pointed out Vanessa Lynch straight away as we walked into the *"Love Coffee"* café in Todmorden. Gazing around, I saw the place was quiet at the moment, just a couple of tables being used, the waitresses, similarly dressed and tattooed to those in the café in Hebden Bridge, standing around and chatting, enjoying what was probably a much-awaited lull between lunchtime and tea time.

It was a cozy little place with a heavily beamed ceiling and dark paneled walls, the oak tables square teamed with heavy chairs with arms and green padded seats and backs. The coffee machine whooshed, creating a fug of steam, and the tantalizing smell of coffee and baking hung in the air as light background music played.

I watched Vanessa as she gazed around self-consciously and then eyes downcast, stirred her cup of coffee with a silver spoon. Her hair was the same amazing frizzy mass and she wore a pair of jeans teamed with a crimson jumper. A thick black coat hung over the back of her chair, and her high-heeled boots, which I could just see beneath the table, were a shiny black.

"Hi, Vanessa Lynch?" I leaned over to peer at her.

She stood up straight away, her eyes wide, a smile curving her lips, "Oh my God, Jenny Clarke. Oh my God," she flung her arms around me and pulled me close, and then stepped back slightly to gaze into my face, "Oh, Jenny, you haven't changed."

"Oh, I don't know," I replied, "I've somehow managed to collect a few grey hairs and wrinkles since I last saw you."

"You were a slip of a girl," she said, "But I'd know you anywhere."

"Even after all these years?" I exclaimed.

"Oh yes, I've never forgotten you."

She peered past me and looked at Andy, who gave a small smile. I moved back a little and said, "Vanessa, this is Andy, um, Andy Valentine."

She opened her eyes even wider, an impossible task I'd thought, but no, they really were wider, and then she gaped at us, her mouth a round O.

"You mean?"

"Yes, Susie's dad."

She held out her hand, "Mr. Valentine, I am so pleased to meet you and so sorry about Susie. Actually, I'm at a loss for words. Please…please sit down, shall we order coffee?"

"Call me Andy," he said as he shook her hand, and we both sat down on the comfortable chairs. "Yes, coffee would be good. It's okay. Sometimes, there just are no words." A waitress glided over and took our order for coffee and cakes. "Walnut would be lovely," Vanessa gushed and then turned to us, "How about you two?"

"I don't mind Battenburg," said Andy, "Is that still a thing?"

"Oh yes," the Waitress replied, "Our Battenburg's very popular."

And then, turning to me, "Jenny?"

"Walnut and Battenburg sound great to me. I'll have a piece of both."

"Very good," said the waitress as she bustled away, clutching her pad and pencil. There was a strange quiet once the waitress had disappeared which I broke by saying, "I'm grateful you agreed to meet us today, Vanessa." And then I laughed a bit, "It seems strange to call you that. I think I used to call you Miss Lynch!"

Vanessa laughed, "Oh yes, you will have done

and, yes, it does seem strange now that we're both older and our ages closer, so to speak."

I nodded and then said, "We wanted to see you because…"

"Yes, the disappearance of Susie Valentine," she said sadly, "Your very first day at the nursery, too, and you bonded so well with her." She drained her coffee and put the cup back on the saucer with a click.

"Yes, I did," I said, "I had massive blank spots in my memory of the day and, well," I glanced at Andy, who gave me a knowing nod, "I've even been to a hypnotist to see if they can be unblocked."

She gazed at me with questions in her eyes, "Did it work?"

"Yes," I nodded and was just about to speak again when the waitress bustled over to the table, pushing a tea trolley from which she deposited our coffee and cakes onto the table. "Enjoy," she said brightly as she trundled away, the trolley wheels squeaking.

"Hmm," said Andy, "Both cakes look delicious, "Shall I be Mother?"

Vanessa gave a delighted chuckle and said, "Please do," as, picking up a knife, he deftly cut into both cakes beautiful wafer-thin slices as Vanessa and I put milk and sugar into our drinks.

"Before you tell me about the hypnotist, Jenny, may I ask you a question?"

"Of course."

"Did you ever become a writer? I know you were dead set on it despite insisting at the end of your work experience that you loved working with children."

I smiled, "Yes, I did enjoy working with children, although what happened to Susie cast a pall over it, but yes, I did become a writer. I've had several novels published."

"Oh my, well, that's great. What do you write? I'd love to have a read."

"They're somewhat spicy," put in Andy, giving me a side-eyed glance.

"Ooh, I must say I do enjoy a bit of spiciness," Vanessa said with a grin.

"Well," I said, "They go by the banner *"Hidden Desires,"* and my pen name is Claudia Raines."

"What a fabulous pen name," Vanessa said, taking a large bite from a slice of walnut cake and munching rapidly, "Claudia Raines. How exciting. Are all your books on Amazon?"

"Yes, Amazon and many other online book stores, including Barnes & Noble and Abe Books." I took a sip of coffee and then reached for the Battenburg.

"I'll have a look," she said, "I'd love to read them." She, too, took a sip of coffee and turned to Andy, "And you, um, Andy, what do you do?"

"I'm on the council, Hebden Royd," he replied,

"The Deputy Clerk."

"Oh, not in Todmorden then?"

"No, I moved to Hebden from Todmorden after Susie disappeared and after my wife and I split up."

"Oh yes, I remember you lived locally," She shook her head sadly, "I think I may have seen you once or twice picking Susie up." She took a gulp of coffee, "I'm so sorry you and your wife split up."

"Yes, the whole thing tore us apart, I'm afraid."

"It's understandable, really."

"What do you do now?" he asked, "Still working with children?"

"No," she replied, shaking her head, tiny little shakes, "Not after that, not after Susie. I felt as if I'd failed everybody that day when it happened."

"Oh no," I said, "But it wasn't your fault."

"No, it wasn't," agreed Andy, "Just everything working against you."

"Susie was in my care," she said, "I had to bear the blame. I resigned and trained to become a Legal Secretary. Oh, I was already a typist, a good fast typist, and the rest came on the job, really. I don't regret it for a second." She picked up a napkin and wiped her fingers, dabbed at her lips, and then poured more coffee, nodding towards the two of us before replenishing our cups.

Andy leaned forward, his elbows on the table,

"Do you remember what happened that day, Vanessa?"

"Yes," she said, "But I told the police everything I know."

"I know," he said, "And I probably heard it from them at the time, but would you tell me?"

She nodded, her eyes suddenly moist as if she could cry. She turned her gaze on me, "You left early that day, didn't you, Jenny?"

"I did, I had an appointment and for the life of me, I can't remember what it was, either the doctor or the dentist."

"The dentist," she said, "I remember it was the dentist. Well, Susie followed you. I saw her wandering around holding on to her daddy's card, saying your name, "Where's Jenny?" she kept saying, "Where's Jenny?"

"Oh no," I blurted out, "I had a feeling that's what might have happened."

"Yes, but don't start blaming yourself, Jenny. Before she actually went out of the door, I guided her back into the main playroom when the phone rang, and I went back into the office to answer it. When I came back, she wasn't in the main playroom, and nobody had seen her. Not even Sonia, the lady that covered for you."

She shook her head, "I remember running frantically in between the two rooms and the toilet area and the cloakroom shouting for Susie. All I could think is that when I went to answer the phone, she sneaked back out of the playroom and went outside. She was so intent on seeing you."

She took a deep breath and then said, "I told Sonia to keep all the other children together while I searched for her. I'll never forget that day, in fact," She looked from one of us to the other, "It's taken on a sort of nightmare scenario. It was blistering hot, and the road was packed with cars. The noise was immense. All I could hear was the beep beep beep of the crossing and the revving of a vehicle nearby, which turned out to be a van, a blue van that suddenly shot past at break-neck speed…"

"A blue van?" I asked her, "That's what I remember too. Registration number 198 NCG." The door pinged, and a couple went out, holding the door open for a large group of people who came in laughing and chattering. They chose a table, and a waitress glided over to take their order.

"I didn't get the registration," said Vanessa, "I was too slow. Oh, how I blame myself, Jenny." She put her hands over her mouth just as the door pinged open again, and another large group of people walked in and, with much scraping of chairs on the floor, settled themselves at a table. The smell of fried food hung in the air, and there was a sizzling sound as if eggs and bacon were cooking. Perhaps the tea-time crowd were on their way.

"You mustn't blame yourself," I said, leaning forward and patting her shoulder, "I only know the registration from being hypnotized, as well as the memory of the blue van parked at the curb, that I saw when I left that day. And I feel guilt, too, now that I know what happened. If Susie hadn't followed me, she wouldn't have gone outside."

Andy put a hand on my arm, "It's not your fault either. Susie must have really taken a shine to you," He squeezed my hand, "She wouldn't have followed you otherwise."

I gave a small smile as I said, "She must have dropped the card she was making, and I picked it up."

"The card?" said Vanessa, leaning in close to myself and Andy, "Jenny…"

"What card?" asked Andy, "What did you find outside?"

"Susie was making a card for you, Andy, a Father's Day card. She must have dropped it when she followed me outside. I found it but must have dropped it as well, and, well, the lady in the yellow dress who I saw when being hypnotized saw me lose it and gave it back to me, and I put it in my rucksack." I looked from Andy to Vanessa, "Emma, my daughter, has my rucksack, but there's no card in it, I'm afraid."

"No," said Vanessa, shaking her head, "It won't be in your rucksack because you gave it to me the following day," She fumbled in her bag, "Look." With a flourish, she produced the card and laid it on the table between us. Andy and I simply stared at it in wonder until Andy said, "May I?"

"Of course," she said. Gently, he picked it up, a great beam of a smile all over his face as he looked at the stick figure on the front of the card. He pointed at it, "I take it this figure is supposed to be me?"

"Yes, I remember her making it as if it was yesterday, her coloring it in, making the eyes very green, oh and her laughing so hard when I said daddy looked cool, and we both sang, *"Daddy cool, daddy cool.* She looked so cute too with a bright red bow in her hair and her dress, um…"

"Her poppy dress," said Andy, "Her favorite, I think."

"Yes, it did have poppies on it. A beautiful dress."

Andy laughed a lot as he repeated again, *"Daddy cool, daddy cool,"* tears coming into his eyes whilst Vanessa delved into her bag again and produced other pictures, saying, "There's more. I kept them all together after the police saw them. Oh, they told me I could keep them, hoping for an opportunity like this to give them back to the parents."

Eagerly, we sifted through them, pictures drawn in pencil, some in felt tip pens, and some in chalk, all on different colored paper and all with a signature of *"Susie Valentine"* and the date. "Look at this one," said Andy, pointing to each stick figure, "Mummy, Daddy, Susie and baby sister. Look at how she's drawn baby sister, just a little dot." He laughed a lot shaking his head, tears coming into his eyes. "These are priceless," he said, "Absolutely priceless."

"Well, they're yours," said Vanessa, as she drained her coffee cup, "Take them home with you, but now I really have to go. I've a big food shop to do for my mum and dad." She handed a carrier bag to Andy, saying, "You might want to put the pictures in here?"

Andy took the bag with a smile, "Thanks for these, Vanessa," he said, nodding at the pictures, "They mean a lot to me."

"It's the least I can do," she replied.

"Wow, you've still got your mum and dad."

"Yes, they're quite frail now, though. That's why I get their shopping." She stood up and shrugged on her coat, picked up her gloves and hat. We stood up too in readiness to go and followed Vanessa outside, waving a cheery goodbye to the waitresses as we left and stepped outside into a rapidly darkening afternoon, the sky navy blue, fluffy white clouds hanging low as if they were a ceiling.

Cars sped past on the busy road, their headlights glowing, and a green double-decker bus pulled up with a screech. Several people stumbled off, looking tired after a long day at work, a couple of passengers going straight into the café, rubbing their hands from the cold, eager for a hot drink and a fry up for tea.

"It's been lovely to see you, Jenny," she said, giving me a hug, "And you, too, Andy. Please do keep in touch."

"We certainly will," I told her as we all shook hands and then stood and watched her as she walked away, her step brisk and her arms swinging at her sides. She stopped and turned once, waving her hand like a little white flag. We waved back until she was almost gone, a tiny black dot in the distance. Andy took my hand and squeezed it tightly within his, "Come on, let's get you safely back to your boat."

"Oh, for a life on the ocean waves," I quipped as we, too, turned and, hunching our shoulders to our ears, hurried down the chilly streets to the car park, Andy holding on tightly to the carrier bag as if it was a lifeline.

"What a great meeting," he said.

"Yes," I agreed, "My memory of Vanessa Lynch is just as I thought it was," And then, "Come home with me? We could have a glass of wine or two."

"Or three? Hmm, do you know, I rather think that sounds like a good idea."

We smiled at each other, and Andy leaned in close and kissed my cheek, his stubble tickling deliciously against my skin. My heart clattering in anticipation, we rushed along the busy streets, our hands joined, our hearts beating in harmony.

***

My phone buzzed on my bedside table, and a text popped up. Leaning closer and narrowing my eyes, I saw it was from Dave, *"Hi Jenny, just checking in. How's things? Will be popping over to your neck of the woods soon. It could well be for Christmas, but more likely Valentine's Day. Would be great to meet up for a Valentine meal and let bygones be bygones, eh?"* I was tired, my eyelids drooping, the land of nod beckoning me, summoning me with the lure of an arched finger. Slowly, I laid down, my head sinking into the pillow, my breathing steadied, and my eyes closed. Just a few deep, luxurious breaths and one last thought, *"Dave's visit here could well be a recipe for disaster,"* and, whoosh, I was gone.

CHAPTER TWELVE

Present Day – Hebden Bridge Christmas Lights Switch On

"Ten, nine, eight, seven, six, five, four, three, two, one," the crowd exploded into a great roar as Santa Claus himself decked out in his beautiful crimson suit, white beard bristling, pressed a bright red button and Hebden Bridge's Christmas lights came on in a great white beam, the massive Christmas tree now a multi-colored glow. Tiny yellow lights twinkled amongst the bushes and trees, and praying angels, the sleeping baby Jesus and the Three Wise Men wearing sumptuous cloaks, swung from lampposts festooned with even more lights in a silvery hue.

It was a frosty night, the paths a slippy silver and the sky a deep black twinkling with tiny stars and the great globe of the moon. The air smelt densely cold, mixed with the acrid smell of frying onions and meaty burgers, sweet candy floss, and sticky toffee apples that quivered in the air like lines of washing. Groups of Morris dancers cavorted merrily, cheered on by the surrounding crowds amidst much howling with laughter as one of the dancers, looking very much like the Chitty Chitty Bang Bang Child Catcher, chased through the crowds with a pig's bladder.

I caught sight of the Town Mayor, Councilor Ronald Rudd, cavorting happily, his rather large belly trembling as Hebden's beautiful regalia clanked around his neck and a flower-laden straw hat tottered on his rather large head like a pea on a drum. People crowded around him, clapping their hands, encouraging him to dance faster, dance harder. Stilt walkers dressed as fairies and elves stood stiff-legged on the sidelines, and a young man strummed an acoustic guitar and sang, his voice echoing around the crowded market square and the packed streets.

Public house doors stood open, customers walking in and out with full and empty glasses, and children, munching on sweets, their faces etched with awe, sat cross-legged in a circle listening to a young woman, her voice high-pitched and excited, reading *"The Snowman."*

I felt a hand on my shoulder and then an arm around my waist, hot breath on my neck, and to my delight, Andy appeared at my side, "That's me finished for the evening. The Clerk's taking over. Do you fancy a drink?"

"Oh yes, that would be lovely."

"The Railway?" I nodded as he grabbed my hand and pulled me through the throngs of people into the public bar of the Railway. Every seat being taken, we queued at the bar until Andy was served with a frothy pint and a glass of red wine.

"Cheers," we said, chinking glasses, people pushing and shoving all around, thrusting us closer and closer together, Andy's chest pressed against my breasts, making my heart clatter harder and harder. It was very warm inside, too, a far cry from the cold frostiness outside, and a fire roared in the old tiled fireplace, red and orange flames licking up the chimney. There was a strong smell of perfume and cigarette smoke that trickled in through the open door. Andy raised his glass to a couple of familiar faces, and the jukebox whirred and clicked, and a disco song from the 1970s blared out, *"Night fever, night fever, we know how to do it …"*

"The Bee Gees," I said happily, "Oh, how good are The Bee Gees?"

"Excellent," replied Andy, "A cause for celebration." We chinked glasses again when, suddenly, something caught my eye at the bar, something that made my heart beat even harder and faster. A man, a bald-headed man. He was turned away from me, his narrow shoulders hunched against a bright white tee shirt tucked into baggy denim jeans, but I had a gut feeling that if he turned around, his face would be wrinkled now, the cross tattoo folded into his cheek and the snake slithering around his neck, caught up in the aged creases. He held a battered-looking black leather jacket in a strong fist.

"Jenny?" Andy shook my arm, "Jenny?"

I came around as if from a dream to look straight into Andy's worried, frowning face, "What is it? You look as if you've seen a ghost."

I leaned in close to him to speak into his ear, "Maybe I have. Please tell me, or am I imagining it? Do you see a bald-headed man standing at the bar?" Andy turned to look, and this time, it was my hand on his arm, as I whispered, "Don't be too obvious," as I looked the other way.

"Yes, I can see a bald-headed man at the bar," The man must have turned his head because Andy suddenly said, "Oh, good God, he's got a black cross tattoo on his cheek."

"Yes," I replied, "And look at his neck."

We could just about make out the head of the snake, little tongue flicked out, beady eyes staring, as it lay motionless close to his ear. I took a sip of wine that shot through my body, relaxing me a little as borne on the crowd around us. We moved a little nearer to the bar and the bald-headed man with the tattoos. He held a pint of beer close to his chest as he spoke to a younger man with a head of thick black hair, a small gold hoop hanging from his ear lobe, and another from his nose. The other man sipped from his pint as he said, "So why don't we get out of here, Albie? I'm getting nothing but hostile stares."

"Take no notice of 'em," growled the bald-headed man, who we now knew was called Albie, "After all, this is a Christmas thing. Peace to all men and what have you."

"Why we didn't stay in Tod tonight, I've no idea."

"Oh, I used to come here, to Hebden, you know, back in the day. Had some good times around here. And anyway," He rounded on the young man, "It's better than the *"Farmer's Arms"* in Tod. It's dead as a doornail in that place!"

"Well, we don't belong here. Too upmarket. Come on." Tipping his head back, the younger man drained his pint as Albie carried on sipping slowly, "Albie, come on," he said urgently.

"Yeah, in my own good time, alright? In my own good time, Ryan." Slowly, he nodded his head up and down, his mouth twisted and his dark eyes daggers. If looks could kill, I certainly wouldn't want to be the young man, Ryan. He had a strange accent too, a mixture of several areas as if he'd traveled around a lot which I suppose he had if he was the man we suspected him to be if he was a gypsy and had owned a blue van, registration number 198 NCG, somebody who was always on the move, going from place to place. Alarmingly easy to snatch a child and hide her away, I suppose.

My stomach rolled alarmingly with horror that this could be the man who had snatched little Susie Valentine, this man standing so close to us, I could almost reach out and touch him. Oh, how I longed to put a firm hand on his shoulder, spin him around, and ask him the question, *"Okay, Albie, where is she? Where's Susie Valentine?"* The whole situation seemed surreal as if I was in a drama or a soap on TV. As if he could read my mind, Andy squeezed my hand and, leaning in close, kissed my cheek and whispered in my ear, "I don't know how I'm managing to keep away from him. If it is him, of course."

"Oh, Andy, it must be, surely. How many bald-headed men have a snake and a cross tattoo, and in the right places, too?"

"Yes, but we've got to be very careful here. No silly moves, you understand what I mean, don't you?"

I nodded as the jukebox suddenly lit up like a Christmas tree, bright primary colors of red, yellow, and blue flashing, and the strains of Donny Osmond singing *"Puppy Love"* rang out. The usual group of rather large men started to sing along, waving their pints in the air, beer spilling from their glasses, oblivious to everything around them. Suddenly, one of the large men stumbled, crashing into the bald man, who lurched forward into the younger man, Ryan, beer spilling between them. Enraged, Albie turned around, still miraculously holding his pint, beer dripping from his tee shirt and his jeans, his arm and hand soaked.

Gripping my hand, Andy said, "Come on, Jenny, let's get out of here. There's going to be trouble." We backed off, crowding into the doorway, as it seemed a million other people were, too, all pushing and shoving and trying to escape. Slowly Albie, put his almost empty glass onto the bar and shouted, his gravelly voice loud, deadly, "Who did that?"

Donny Osmond's voice faded away, and with a whirr and a click, the record came to an end, and the jukebox fell silent, just the lights flashing lozenges of color. The group of large men stood motionless, shiftily looking from one to the other, their eyes not meeting, as people still tried to get out of the doorway, elbowing each other out of the way as if their lives depended on it.

The landlord rapped on the bar, "Calm down, ladies and gents, calm down now. There's no harm done."

He turned to Albie and the young man, Ryan, "Alright now, Sir, finish your pint, and then maybe it's time to leave." The whole pub fell into a silence so deep, you could hear a pin drop, everybody waiting with bated breath until Albie broke it, his voice ringing out, "I ain't going nowhere. It weren't my fault," His neck bulged with the effort of shouting, the tattooed snake swelling up as if it had eaten something very large. A crocodile, perhaps?

"Okay then, Sir," said the landlord, pulling a mobile phone from his pocket, "I'll call the police, eh?" Rapidly he tapped some numbers onto the keyboard and put it to his ear.

The young man with the earrings grabbed Albie's upper arm, "Come on, Albie, let's go. We don't want no trouble, okay?"

Slowly, deliberately, Albie put his pint glass to his lips and drained it, staring around with his dark eyes whilst he placed it on the bar and shrugged into his leather jacket, pulling the collar up, obscuring the snake from prying eyes. He swaggered towards the doorway, closely followed by the young man, as the relieved crowds parted, like Jesus parting the red sea, to let them go, watching them and whispering amongst themselves all the derogatory words they could think of, which, with the threat of the police hanging over his head, Albie decided was best to ignore.

Outside, Andy and I watched them go, two figures wandering away across the Market Square until they became two black dots. With a sudden thought, I drained my wine and said, "Andy, we should follow them. Don't you think?"

He didn't answer at first but just stared after them, his eyes narrowed as if he was thinking hard, "Yes, you're right, Jenny. Come on." Leaving our glasses on a table, we set off after them, picking up our speed, trying to keep close but not too close, as they swaggered unsteadily into the cold, clear night, the crowds thinning out now as we left all the music and lights behind us.

***

I woke up all of a sudden, breathing heavily, too warm under the thick quilt, disorientated for a split second, and wondering where I was. Until I realized, with a sense of relief, that I was at home, safely in my bed on my boat. I was aware of Sydney's light breathing, her body moving up and down, a tight, curled ball at my side. Sitting up a little and reaching out an arm, I located my phone and took a quick glance at the screen, which was empty, blank. Laying back down, thoughts of Andy ran through my mind as I remembered the evening before and all that had happened after we'd followed the man, Albie, and his friend, Ryan. But first of all, dear reader, needs must and a hot reviving cup of coffee was next on the agenda, after which, I would tell all.

Carefully, so as not to disturb the sleeping cat, I quietly swung my legs out of bed and, shrugging on a dressing gown, padded out to the kitchen, where I flicked on the kettle and peered from the tiny window as it purred to a boil. The day was sunny, the sky blue speckled with snowy clouds, but it was windy, the trees bowing and scraping, their branches shaking, and leaves flying through the air, crimson, and orange. Even the canal water was choppy, ducks and geese and swans riding the tiny waves.

Going back to bed, I made myself comfortable, a pillow at my lower back, sipping at the hot coffee as Sydney woke up and began to head-butt my arm, purring happily. I stroked her tiny soft head as she stood on my lap, kneading with her paws, and my mind wandered back to last night and what had happened when Andy and I had followed the bald man, Albie, and his side-kick, Ryan.

"I have a feeling I know where they're going, Andy, don't you?" I remember saying, and Andy nodding, "Yeah, the field behind Brush Row in Todmorden."

We watched as the two men stopped at a wagon parked at the curb. It definitely wasn't a blue van but an open-backed wagon filled to the brim with all sorts of scrap metal, battered washing machines, discarded ovens and fridges, metal curtain poles, all higgledy-piggledy thrown together, its cab a bright sunny yellow. They set off quickly, tires squealing, and once again, the thought, *"I wouldn't want to be the young man, Ryan, with Albie driving in a bad mood,"* flashed through my mind.

Once the wagon had gone, Andy and I made our way to the Town Hall, where his car was parked, and set off from there, the car's headlights a bright white glow lighting up the dark streets, fervently hoping we were right about where the two men were heading to. We soon caught up with them and tailed them at a steady pace, countryside and buildings all going past in a blur until we arrived at Brush Row, and the wagon indicated left to drive straight through a pair of wide-open metal gates into the field behind Emma's house destined someday to contain yet more houses. The wagon stopped, and the younger man, Ryan, hopped out and carefully closed the gates.

"I hope he hasn't locked those gates," I said, as Andy pulled up at the curb, cut the engine, and turned off the lights. I eyed the houses and caught sight of Emma's, where a rosy red glow shone in the sitting room window, and a lamp shone from baby Milly's room. A shadow flickered behind the curtains, and I imagined it being Emma or Jack holding the baby, rocking her to sleep, or feeding her a bottle.

"I bet you'd love to pay your daughter a visit, eh, Jenny?" Andy smiled, his handsome face a maze of wrinkles and dimples, his lips red and full, and his eyes a deep veiled green. My stomach lurched at the thought of my lips touching his, but I took a deep breath and tried to concentrate on the job at hand.

I nodded, "Oh yes, I would, but let's see what this Albie is up to first, eh?"

He nodded as quietly we stepped from the car, both of us glad we'd worn dark clothing, as we zipped up our jackets and put up our hoods, even though there was no rain and the evening was still cold and dry, stars twinkling in a midnight blue sky and the moon just a slither now like a slit in the Heavens. Softly, we walked along the pavement and approached the gates, my heart beating hard, dreading them being locked, but, on a gentle push, one opened, allowing us to slip through and step into the field.

There were caravans dotted about all over the place. The grass around them churned up now with tire marks. Washing lines had been erected with dilapidated poles and what looked like garden twine, and washing still hung out, pairs of jeans, tee shirts, towels, and sheets, blowing a little in the breeze eerie as phantoms in the dark. Great barbecue pits had been dug into the earth and children's toys and bikes were scattered about, empty chocolate and sweet wrappers lying amongst them.

There was even a children's swing and slide made of thick heavy plastic, a makeshift playground. A couple of skinny dogs roamed around on long silver chains, and there were others eating from bowls or drinking from muddy puddles, and cats, too, slinking through the dark, their eyes shining like lamps or sitting cleaning themselves with their tiny pink tongues. The smell of cooking rose into the air, fried fish and chips, the cheesy odor of pizza, and the meatiness of burgers or sausages.

We crept around the edge of the field, keeping close to the fence and making sure our heads were down and well hidden in our hoods. I saw the upstairs light go off in Emma's house and smiled at the thought of Milly fast asleep in her cot while Emma and Jack snuggled on the sofa watching TV.

"Jenny? Look," Andy pointed with a finger as he whispered, "There's the wagon." And then added, "Maybe a replacement for the blue van."

"Yes, it's newer, isn't it?

"I saw the registration number earlier. It's ALB YL51, which I take to be part of his name, you know, the ALB, and the rest is a 2000 number."

"Wow, it might be newer than the old van but it's parked up outside the most dilapidated caravan, don't you think?"

Andy chuckled as we looked at the caravan. At the bright light shining through the ragged curtains and the smoke pouring from its little chimney, the crackle of food being fried, and the murmur of a television. My mind racing, I thought of little Susie being brought to this very caravan, taken away from her mum and dad, her nursery, and all she knew. A great sadness overwhelmed me when a noise sounded to the side of us, a rustling in the bushes and a growl, a soft warning growl.

Andy squeezed my hand in his as I whispered, "Oh God, I hope one of those dogs hasn't escaped from its chain. They looked quite mean and hungry, if you get my drift." And then there was a voice, making my heart race, "Ssh, Bruno, come here," And then, "No! Bruno!"

Making us both step back in horror, a large dog suddenly ran at us, a German Shepherd I think, although I'm no expert, all bristling fur and big teeth. I lost my footing and fell backwards onto the muddy, rutted ground, the dog standing over me, alternately barking and growling. As brave as a warrior, Andy stepped in front of the dog and caught hold of my hand, pulling me up just as a woman appeared. She was scantily dressed for November, wearing only shorts and a vest top, her legs bare and heavily mottled, an unzipped fleecy cardigan for warmth, and dirty trainers on her feet. She shouted at the dog to *"come here immediately,"* which it did, stepping back yet keeping a wary eye on us, a low rumble in its throat.

"Are you okay, Jenny?" Andy asked, his face etched with concern, his hand very warm in mine.

I nodded as I brushed down my coat, afraid now that we'd alerted attention to ourselves and people here would ask questions because if they did, I had simply no idea what we would say.

"Who are you?" the woman asked, keeping well back and holding tightly to the dog's collar.

"You don't know us," said Andy, "But we're looking for somebody."

Giving Andy a quick glance, I said, "Yes, we're looking for somebody called Albie?"

"Why?" asked the woman. Her pretty face, framed with thick dark hair, looked wary, "What do you want with him?"

"Oh, just to talk to him," I said, "Um, I have a feeling I know him from way back." I was stammering, making a fool of myself I just knew it.

"Albie Shelby?" she asked.

"Is that the man with the snake tattoo on his neck?" asked Andy, "And a tattoo on his face too?"

"Albie Shelby?" I thought, "A rhyming name? No, never!" Nervous laughter bubbled up inside me.

"Yeah, that's him. I don't know what possessed him," She shrugged, "Although he was young when he got the tattoos done." And then, as an aside, "Put me off getting any though."

We all smiled, and Andy said, "You're in the minority then."

"You're right there," She replied as she kept hold of the dog's collar, even though he was straining hard and trying to get away. God help us all if he did.

She giggled a bit and then, perhaps noticing my scared face said, "Oh, don't worry about Bruno, he won't hurt you. Soft as a brush, he is. He's protecting me, that's all."

"Well," I said with a nervous grin, "Forgive me if I can't agree with you at the moment."

"Here, look," She let the dog go, and I panicked, raising my arms into the air, but Bruno simply sat back on his haunches, looking at the woman with a soft brown gaze as she gave him treats, "Good boy," she said, "Good boy, Bruno."

She giggled again and said, "I could probably get you a meet with Albie."

My heart rose, and I gave Andy a sideways glance as the woman carried on, "Albie's my dad. I'm Anita Shelby, well Anita Warner since I got married. You're not reporters, are you? From the local rag?"

"No, we're not reporters," I shook my head,

"Why would we be?"

"Oh, reporters are always wanting a scoop on us. You know we're gypsies right, and not supposed to be here? We're holding up building works, apparently." She shrugged.

A hot wave of annoyance washed over me at the thought, *"Hmm, they know exactly what they're doing,"* but I said calmly, "No, it's nothing like that. We'd just like a word with Albie, that's all."

My phone pinged, bringing me out of my reverie, and everything disappeared, the muddy, rutted field, the caravans, the washing blowing on the lines, the growling dog, and the woman called Anita Shelby. Taking a deep breath, I picked up my phone, dreading a text from Dave, but it was from Andy, *"Morning Jenny. Wow, what a night, eh? Ring me when you can."*

Without hesitation, I tapped on Andy's number and put my phone to my ear. It buzzed for a second or two, and then I heard Andy's lovely voice.

"Hi, morning Jenny. Okay, so where do we go from here then?"

CHAPTER THIRTEEN

Present Day - "Hidden Desires"

"The pub was packed, people queuing three deep at the bar, the air was very hot, and the smell of perfume ripely seductive. Music played very loud, old disco hits from the seventies making Josh want to dance and sing and raise his arms in the air. Henry grinned at him and placed a warm hand on his shoulder.

"Hey, isn't that your ex over there, Jeanette? Was that her name?"

My head snapped around, and yeah, Henry was right. It was Jeanette looking as gorgeous as ever in a tight-fitting black dress, the neckline low, showing far too much flesh. "Flesh," I thought with a pang, "That used to be mine." She'd piled her hair up on top of her head, showing off her pretty neck, "long as a gazelle's," I thought, remembering the kisses I used to rain all over her smooth skin, inhaling her scent as my lips moved slowly, so slowly.

"I'll get the drinks, yeah," whispered Henry very

close into my ear, sending a shiver down my spine, "Seems to me you can't tear your eyes away from Jeanette's charms, eh?"

Pulling myself back into the present, I said, "Hey," I'll get them," as I pushed in front of him, "What'll it be?"

"Martini, shaken but not stirred," he said in an overly deep voice, reminiscent of Bond and of Sean Connery saying, my name's Bond, James Bond, making me smile. God, there was no more ready wit than Henry's. Jeanette might be beautiful, but did she have a wit like Henry's? I was confused, my feelings all over the place…"

"Hmm, now, where was I going with this?" My mind raced, wondering now which route to take. I was digging a hole, that's for sure. I shivered, wrapping my blanket tighter around my body, and looking reproachfully at the wood-burning stove, and wishing it could light itself. Maybe if I stared at it for long enough, a miracle might happen? Um, no! The thought of going out onto the deck for a new bag of coal in this weather was unthinkable.

Yeah, living on a barge in the winter was no fun, although, I had to admit, it still held a strange kind of beauty, especially at the moment. My eyes were drawn to the window where I could see snowflakes falling softly from a low white sky, settling peacefully on the towpath and decorating the window with its beautiful patterns, their names of Fern Frost and Ice Flowers equally as beautiful.

Most of the birds had disappeared, their crazy noise and antics gone for the winter, but a few hardy ones were still there, standing at the water's edge, their heads tucked into their wings. Sydney knew they were there and had enjoyed many a summer day staring at them with her greedy cat's eyes, but it was even too cold for her today, and she was curled up beside me, a tiny pulsating ball, snuffling in her sleep.

My phone began to vibrate, moving up and down on the table like a wild thing, and, looking at the screen, I saw *"Emma calling,"* so happily I picked it up. "Hello?"

"Mum, how are you?"

"Yeah, absolutely fine, cold, but absolutely fine. How's my little granddaughter?"

"She's absolutely fine, too, and oh, I had a word last night with Jack about Christmas Day at Andy's, and he's up for it. So kind of Andy."

"That's great. Apparently, he cooks a mean roast turkey. I can't wait."

"Neither can I. Now, look, Mum, what are you and Andy going to do now?"

"You mean about this Albie fella? I take it they're all still on the field?"

"Well, yes, they are. There's no moving them for a while, and certainly not in this weather."

"Maybe they intend to stay for Christmas and then move on?"

"Yeah, could be, I hope so. Oh, Mum, I used to love looking out at that field. So beautiful when it snowed and there were no marks on it, totally pristine white, just ready for someone to walk all over and leave footprints."

"You mean you, Emma?"

She giggled and said, "Yeah, me, I just couldn't resist, but now, well, it's covered with stuff, caravans, kid's toys, litter. The snow all trodden on and brown."

"I know, but they'll be going at some point, which means Andy and I will have to move fast before he's gone forever, and we never find out what happened to Susie."

"So, what are you going to do, then?"

I took a deep breath, "Why, contact the police, of course."

Emma gave a great sigh, "I'm really glad, Mum, that's definitely the best thing to do."

"Yes, we've talked it over, and we think it is, Emma."

We said our goodbyes, and I clicked off my mobile and just sat thinking for a moment or two, realizing there was somebody else who needed to know about this as well. Resolutely I tapped in another number and put my phone to my ear. I watched the snow falling as it rang and rang, a childish excitement coursing through me at the thought of a white Christmas. "Hello? Vanessa? It's Jenny. Yes, I'm fine. I'm ringing because, well, there's something you should know."

***

A Couple of Days Before

"So, can you introduce us to your dad?" I asked Anita Shelby. The dog, Bruno, sat at her side, gazing up at her, imploring her to give him more treats because he was a good dog, really. He'd had to bark at the nasty people, hadn't he? He was only doing his duty and protecting her, as any well-behaved doggy would.

"Well, I can't disturb him now. It's a bit late for him, but if you give me your phone number, I'll arrange something."

Andy and I exchanged glances, both of us I knew reluctant to give our phone numbers to just anybody, particularly somebody we'd only just met, but, and this was a big but, if Albie agreed to meet with us, this could be an enormous breakthrough. If we wanted information on Susie, we really had no choice.

"Okay," I said, "Are you sure we can't have a quick word with him now, though?"

"No," she shook her head, "He's getting on a bit you know, likes to get his head down early. No late nights up carousing for him no more." She giggled and looked from one of us to the other. "Well?"

"Okay, you can have mine," said Andy. Producing a phone from the back pocket of her shorts, Anita tapped his number in, saying, "Right, I'll get back to you as soon as I speak to Dad." And with that she was off, the dog Bruno chasing after her, barking happily, a lovely family dog and not a killing machine as we'd first thought.

"Damn," I said, "Oh, Andy do you think we've been duped?"

He shook his head, "I don't know, Jenny. I hope not. She seemed fairly sincere, don't you think?" He gazed at me wryly before saying, "Come on, let's go back to the car. It's cold and dark. Time to get home."

Linking arms, we made our way out of the metal gates, hurrying now as a fine rain had begun to fall, and we burrowed into our hoods, trying to keep out the icy cold, when a figure stepped out from the shadows right in front of us, and said, "Got a fag?"

A dart of fear shot through me, but peering through the rain and darkness, I could see it was a woman of a similar age to Anita, dressed in dark denim jeans. She also wore a jacket with no hood and her hair was wet, plastered to her scalp. With no hat, scarf, or gloves, it was no wonder her face was pinched with cold, her nose red.

"No, I'm sorry," I said, "Neither of us smoke." We made to move on, but she stopped us by saying, "Were you just talking to Anita Warner? Well, Shelby that she was?"

"Yes, do you know her?"

"Know her? I should say. She's my cousin, my dad's Albie's brother. I know her sister, too. Oh, I'm Ruth, by the way, Ruth Shelby."

"Nice to meet you, Ruth," We said in unison, even holding out our hands to shake hers, "So you're still a Shelby then?"

"Oh yes, never been married, never had kids. Didn't want to, thought I could be a successful single woman, but look at me now, begging for cigarettes from strangers." She gave a rueful grin and then said, "Maybe I could have done better, eh?"

It was difficult to know what to say to that, so instead, I said, "Shall we move under the trees over there? It'll provide some shelter while we talk. We're all getting soaked."

They both nodded and followed me across the road, where we stood in a huddle, still a bit chilly but at least protected and dry. "You said Anita had a sister? So, she's your cousin as well, isn't she?"

"Well, no, not legally like."

"Legally?"

"Look, I could tell you all sorts about that family

if I only had a fag."

"Sorry, but," Andy hesitated for a split second and then reached into his pocket for his wallet from where he produced a ten-pound note and handed it to her. "Get yourself a pack," he said.

She took it, snatching it from his hand and putting it carefully in her pocket. "Thanks, but they cost twelve pounds a packet, now you know."

"Really?" He said as he fumbled in his pocket for change and handed her a couple of pound coins, "Daylight robbery!"

"You're telling me," She replied as she pocketed the coins, "Now then, Anita's sister ain't my real cousin as such because she was adopted."

A surge of something like dread shot through my body at the word "adopted," and as the girl carried on speaking, the feeling got stronger and stronger, "Uncle Albie's wife died in childbirth, both her and the baby, only young she was, it was so sad, the baby was a little boy, and Uncle Albie was distraught. Oh my God, so distraught. He already had a daughter, that's Anita, who you spoke to, so he found himself a single parent to an eight-year-old. Good dad he was, though, took great care of her."

A breeze suddenly sprang up, shaking the trees and raining down icy drops that soaked us through. Despite that, Andy and I stayed, hunched into our coats, mesmerized by the woman's story. She carried on, "One day though, he comes home with this little girl, a little tot, tells us he adopted her, all through the proper channels and all, but, well, even my mum and dad were suspicious, and they love Uncle Albie. Us kids used to take the mick out of him, you know, singing at him, *"Albie Shelby, Albie Shelby,"* ooh, he really hated that." She stared into the middle distance, reminiscing, I suppose.

"What were your mum and dad suspicious of?" I asked, "It is possible for single men to adopt and, as he lost a child and his wife, maybe he," I shrugged, "Just longed for another?"

"Yeah, I get what you're saying, but he hadn't mentioned anything about adopting before, and there's lots of channels to go through. It all takes time. You don't just pop off one day and come home with a child. Even Anita knew nothing about it, and you'd have thought he would have told her she was gonna have a sister."

She sighed, "Think about it, he just turned up with this little girl, and even I thought it was strange, and I was only nine. And as well as that, we all had to move on then, out of the area, and we didn't come back here for years. She's okay though, the little girl, married now and everything, even got a couple of kids. Both boys."

"So, she's here?" asked Andy, "Still living with all of you here on the field?" His voice sounded shocked, disbelieving. As if such a thing could never happen.

She nodded, "Yeah."

"When did this happen?" I asked her, "When did Albie bring the little girl home?" A strange sense of foreboding settling through my body, I reached for Andy's hand and squeezed it hard.

"Nineteen ninety," she said, "It was summer, I remember, and really hot and sunny. He said she was called June. I don't know whether she was already called that or he re-named her, but she's answered to that ever since.

There was a brief silence before she spoke again, her tone angry, "So if you are from the local rag, like Anita thought you were, you can publish my story. I don't care who knows, I've always thought it odd, him turning up like that with a little girl, and I've got more and more upset about it over the years. Go ahead and publish it. I'd even tell the police if you want me to."

"We're not from the press," I said gently, "But we do have an interest in your story…"

"You know who the little girl is, don't you?"

"Perhaps," said Andy, "But we can't say any more at the moment, but thank you for this, for telling us your story."

"What did she look like?" I asked her.

"What, June?" She shrugged, "Pretty little thing, cute face, dark hair, greeny color eyes."

"Dark hair?"

"Yeah, straight dark hair to her shoulders."

Andy sounded defeated as he said, "Well, thanks Ruth. You've been more than helpful."

"Why didn't you go to the police with your suspicions?" I asked her.

She shook her head, "Oh God no, I'd have been in real trouble. It's best someone else does it. It would have been seen as a betrayal of the family, and I was too young then anyway, I didn't think."

"But isn't telling us a betrayal of the family?" asked Andy.

"He won't know, will he? Unless you tell him that is, and, anyway, I know better now." She gave us a suspicious, assessing glare.

Andy and I exchanged a glance, "We're saying nothing," Andy replied, "But what if we told the police and they wanted to speak to you?"

"Well, that's okay. That way, I didn't actually go to the police myself. Do you see what I mean?"

We nodded, and I said, "Now go back to your caravan. You're soaked through."

"Nah," She gave us a cheeky grin, "I'm off to the shop first, gotta get me fags. Thanks again." She walked away, her shoulders hunched to her ears, water dripping from her hair and flowing like little rivers down her face.

"Oh, Ruth," said Andy, walking after her, "Just one more thing. Sorry."

She turned around, "Yeah?"

"Which is June's caravan?"

"Um, well, it's not far from Albie's and Anita's. It's painted green. Very well put together is their place, they're both a bit fussy."

"Who's her husband?" My heart felt tight and squeezed at the beseeching look on Andy's face.

"Oh, he's a friend of Ryan's, Ryan's one of Albie's grandsons, Anita's boy. He came along to help out one time," She shrugged, "And never left. Took a shine to June straight away, I think." She laughed.

"Ah, Ryan," I said, "He was the young man with Albie in the pub in Hebden."

"Yeah, they often drink together. Anything else?"

"What's her husband's name?"

"Bob," she replied, "Bob Edwards and their two boys are Bobby and Vince."

"Thank you," he said, and then again, "Thank you, Ruth."

Andy gripped my hand as we resumed our hurried walk to the car, "Good God, Jenny, I thought we were on to something there, but the child had dark hair. Susie was blonde." He gave a great sigh.

"Albie could have put a wig on her. Don't forget, Susie had her hair in pigtails that day. Ruth just said that the girl's hair was straight to her shoulders. Could easily have been a wig."

Andy looked hopeful again, "Yeah, you're right, Susie did have her hair in pigtails, I remember Fran doing her hair that morning, but, even so, we've landed ourselves in it, haven't we, by speaking with Anita, and even so, what on earth do we do now? Speak to this, Albie, you know, do it on our own, so to speak, or go to the police?"

"Yeah, if Anita tells Albie about us, he might guess what we want to talk about, but then again, because he got away with it for so long, he might not. I think telling the police is the only thing to do, really."

Once in the car, Andy turned up the heater as I took off my gloves and my hat and tried to shake the wet out of them. I shook my head sadly, "Makes me wonder why the police didn't find her at the time. It's so terrible. Such a waste."

Andy shrugged as he indicated and drove away from the curb. "I don't know who they questioned at the time, everything's a blur, but Albie probably wouldn't have been in the picture. Not with him upping sticks and traveling around all the time."

"Yes, you could be right, but most things tie up, the dates for example, him calling the little girl, June, the month he "adopted" her. It's got to be him, Andy."

"Yes, most of it does tie up, Jenny, but, well, it's too good to be true. I can't let myself believe it, in case I'm disappointed."

I squeezed his hand, "I don't know how you keep so patient. Some people would go straight to Albie's caravan and have it out with him."

Andy shook his head, "What, and show everybody that I'm no better than him? No, I'm biding my time. If Susie is there somewhere, I want her as she is now, a woman, to meet a dad she can be proud of."

I reached out and squeezed his hand, loving every word he'd said. He gave me a sideways smile and a gentle wink and then looked forward, his eyes on the road, as he drove carefully all the way home.

***

"Hi Jenny, Dave here checking in. It's getting really close to that oh so wonderful time of the year again, Christmas! I've loads of extra work over the yuletide, so I will give your neck of the woods a temporary miss. Definitely be there for Valentine's Day, though. I'll be the guy hidden behind the ginormous bouquet of red roses, lol. I'll come and find you, okay? Have a lovely Christmas, darling, on your little love boat. Thinking of you xxx

***

"Hi, Jenny. I've just had a voicemail from Anita Shelby saying she had a word with her dad, and he says (these are his own words apparently), "No way, I ain't talking to no one. Tell 'em to get lost!" So, there we have it. No joy from him, eh? Something to hide, don't you think? I'll see you tonight. I'm looking forward to a Christmas Eve drink with you. Ax

"Hmm, I hadn't expected Albie Shelby to welcome us with open arms (his name still felt weird to say. Methinks Albert Shelby definitely has more of a ring to it), so it was great we'd found out most of what we needed to know from Ruth Shelby. A visit to the gypsy camp with the police would be far more helpful to us than sneaking around on our own and being attacked by what appeared to be a vicious dog (even though Bruno turned out to be a sweetheart) and almost causing a bad injury falling backwards onto a churned up muddy field.

My heart rose at the thought of Andy being reunited with his long-lost daughter. That was if she wanted to be reunited. Some did and some didn't. And there was another thing, something I'd never say to Andy, but would she even remember him? Childhood memories don't always go back very far. Mine were a blank before the age of about five. I tapped on reply to his message.

"Hi Andy, I didn't think we'd get much from Albie

Sheldon, so yes, I think we can come to the conclusion that he does have something to hide. Looking forward to tonight. Christmas Eve, here we come! Shall I meet you in the pub? Jx

And two minutes later, *"Yes, the Railway. I can't wait to see you Ax."*

CHAPTER FOURTEEN

Present Day – the weird time in between Christmas and New Year

"Hello?"

I could just about hear a tinny voice, "Good morning, Todmorden Police Station."

"Yes, good morning, I have a crime to report. Could you please tell me who I should speak to?"

I watched him as, holding his phone to his ear, he listened to the tinny voice, his face somber, "It's a historical crime from nineteen ninety concerning the disappearance of Susie Valentine."

He listened again, "Of course. My address is 16 Spring Villas, Hebden Bridge. Thank you, I'll be here."

We were in Andy's house, a beautiful Victorian terrace, set on a hill that climbed vertically from Hebden Bridge out onto the moor, or "the tops" as the locals call it, a far cry from my little boat as the house boasts fine large rooms with high ceilings, a large cellar filled with vintage wine (a couple of bottles of which we sampled on Christmas Day) and attics with ancient buzzers to call the maids to their duties, in the days when servants were a thing. There was just a small yard at the front of the house but a large lawned garden at the back, complete with massive old trees and bushes.

"They're sending an officer out, Jenny." He began to pace the room, "Oh, what have I done? What if it's not her? Oh God, I..." The dog, Ziggy, whined, aware that Andy was upset, so he hunkered down and gently stroked Ziggy's head before resuming his pacing.

"Andy, please stop worrying. It's got to be her; everything points to it."

"No," he said, "Not everything," He shook his head, "Susie was blonde. The child Albie Shelby took home was dark-haired."

"That's the only thing that doesn't tally, and, as I've said before, she could have been wearing a wig. It seems he's wily enough to do that if he thought he could get away with it. The dates tally, the name he gave her, June, tallies. I saw the man, Albie, when I was hypnotized, and Susie followed me outside, so she was there too. Please, Andy, stop pacing and come here," I held out my arms, and dutifully, he stopped pacing and walked straight into my embrace.

"Calm down," I whispered as I pulled him close and rubbed his back with the palm of my hand, "Just tell them everything you know. They'll question Albie and, well, we'll see what happens then."

Taking deep, calming breaths and pulling me even closer, he said, "Has Vanessa been in touch with you?"

"Yes, I said we'd contact her after we'd spoken to the police."

He nodded, "Yes, that's a good idea." And then heartfelt, "Oh, Jenny, I'm so glad I met you." He pulled away, holding me at arm's length, staring at me as if I was a study, a muse. His eyes roamed my face, looking carefully at my mouth, my nose, into my eyes, his gaze traveling to my hair, "You're so beautiful." His mouth hovered over mine, red and ripe as a strawberry, teasing me, tantalizing me, when the doorbell buzzed, a harsh, angry sound, and we both jumped out of our skin.

He swallowed hard before saying, "Oh my God, that was quick. I didn't think they'd get here so soon."

"Yes, just goes to show how important this case still is and that there's still hope." And when he stood there motionless and the bell buzzed again, "You'd better answer the door, Andy."

"Yes, yes, of course."

He fled from the room, and I heard the door

open and his voice, "Good morning, officers, please, come through." I heard the tramp of feet along the tiled floor of the hallway, and I took a deep breath and faced the doorway, my heart thumping in my breast as I waited for the police to enter.

***

"Mum, will you please pick up your phone. I've rung three times this morning, sent a couple of texts and now I'm leaving this voicemail. I don't know when you're seeing the police, but they're packing up, the gypsys, I mean, they're going. When the last one has gone, I'm putting Milly in the car, and I'm going to follow them. It looks as if the building work will go ahead a lot sooner than we thought. Oh, Mum, get in touch. Please!"

***

"Well, first things first," said Detective Inspector Jack Rand, "We'll need a warrant to speak to this er," He consulted his notes, "Albie Shelby." Both police officers were flecked with snow, white flakes like dandruff that were rapidly thawing and dripping onto the carpet. I'd made coffee and they sat comfortably on the settee, each with a mug balanced on their knees, a plate of biscuits on the coffee table in front of them.

"But, how long will that take?" asked Andy, his face seeming to fold in on itself in sheer disappointment.

"From a few hours to a few days," said the Inspector, "Leave it with us." He nodded towards his side-kick, Sergeant Ben Lofthouse, who stood up as the Inspector did, tidily putting their mugs down, to take their leave. We'd told them everything we knew about the bald-headed man called Albie Shelby and what his niece, Ruth Shelby, had told us about the little "adopted" girl turning up at the caravan in the exact same month and year that Susie Valentine had gone missing.

"But they might move on," said Andy, "They're gypsies, they don't stay in the same place for too long, you know. Oh, and they're there illegally and holding up building work."

"We're well aware of that, Sir," replied the Detective Inspector, "But, well, there's a lot of red tape with this sort of thing. I'll try to get a warrant for today."

I put in a point, "Now that Albie Shelby knows there's somebody wanting to speak to him because of what we said to his daughter, Anita, he might just do that, move on, I mean. If he does, he'll make sure to move as far away as possible, and we might never find him again."

"And as well as that," put in Andy, "The little girl, Susie, a grown woman now, has a caravan of her own with her own family, so maybe you won't need a warrant just to speak to Mr. Shelby or his daughter, Anita."

"Yes, you have a valid point there," replied the Sergeant.

Carefully, the Detective Inspector picked up his trilby hat from the coffee table and placed it on his head. He was a smart man wearing a black suit, a snowy white shirt, and highly polished black shoes. "My hands are tied without a warrant," he said, "It's for protection as much as anything, but don't worry, Mr. Valentine, if he runs, we'll find him wherever he decides to go. I've got both your mobile numbers so myself and Sargeant Lofthouse here will be in touch."

Sergeant Ben Lofthouse suddenly spoke up, "We had no reason to question this er, Albie Shelby at the time, Mr. Valentine, so it seems we had no actual proof to charge him anyway. No previous or anything."

"But look at what we've told you today," said Andy, "Surely all that information warrants some action. You must speak to his daughter, Ruth. She told us what we're telling you. She even said we could go to the press, and we know Mr. Shelby was outside the nursery when Susie went missing."

The Sergeant cleared his throat, "With all due respect, Sir," He motioned towards me with a hand, "Mrs. Clarke only saw this under hypnosis. There's no real memory."

"My memories came to the fore because of the hypnosis," I said cuttingly.

"Come on now," said the Detective Inspector, raising a warning hand, "There's no need for that, Sergeant Lofthouse. I'm sure Mrs. Clarke knows what she saw under hypnotism or not."

"We've since found out, Mr. Shelby lost his wife and son, officers, perhaps he was," I shrugged and glanced at Andy, "Mentally affected, depressed, when he did what he did."

"Maybe, Mrs. Clarke. However, we will take action today if possible. As I said before, we've got your mobile numbers and will be in touch."

Giving a nod of his head, he and the Sargeant walked towards the door, Andy behind them, dragging his feet, but ready to open the door for them and see them off, watch them walk down the garden path, get into their car and drive away without a backward glance.

Shaking my head with a sense of defeat, I went to the kitchen where my phone was charging, its screen blank until I pulled out the plug and several items flashed up onto the screen. My heart beat fast, and I saw a host of missed calls from Emma, texts, and a voicemail. Quickly, I tapped on a text, *"Mum, they're moving. I'm going to follow them. Please get in touch."*

Rushing into the sitting room, I shouted, "Andy, get the Detective Inspector back. They're moving quickly."

"Moving?" asked Andy, bewildered, "Who's moving?"

"The gypsies, Albie Shelby," I waved my phone, "I've had loads of messages from Emma. She's going to follow them."

I heard a shout from Andy as he rushed out of the door, but it was too late. The police car had gone, bouncing down the cobbled street on its way back to Todmorden. Putting my mobile to my ear, I rang Emma who, thanks to hands free, answered immediately, "Mum, at last, where have you been?" I could barely hear her for the sound of traffic screeching past and the wind howling like ghosts.

"I'm so sorry, Emma, we've been talking to the police, and my phone was charging. What's happening? Is Milly okay?"

"Of course, she's sleeping peacefully right here next to me. What are the police going to do?"

"They need a warrant to speak to Albie Shelby. They were just leaving Andy's place when I saw your messages. Andy tried to stop them, but it was too late. They're on their way back to Todmorden."

"Oh, mum, if Albie suspects you're on to him, they could go miles away."

"I know. Where are you now? Can you see them?"

"Yes, I can see a whole convoy of caravans. A bit

like that film *"Truckers,"* She giggled, "I'm on the A58 heading towards Manchester. There's a place there for travelers to stay, it's near the city center, I think. Maybe you could take a look at Google Maps."

"Okay, we're heading your way. I'll ring the police from the car to tell them what's happened. Try to keep them in sight, Emma, or ring me if they go off course."

"Will do, Mum."

"Oh, and drive carefully. It might be icy."

We clicked off and Andy and I shrugged on our coats and pulled up our hoods as it was still snowing, fine flakes hovering in the air beneath a low white sky, settling rapidly on the paths and the roads. Andy locked the door firmly behind us as quickly as we could. Slipping and sliding, we hurried out to the car.

***

"Good morning, Todmorden Police Station."

"Hello, good morning. Could I speak to Detective Inspector Jack Rand, please?"

"I'll see if he's in his office. May I ask who's calling?"

"It's Jenny Clarke. We've just been talking to him about the Susie Valentine case."

"Hold the line a moment, please, Mrs. Clarke."

There was a lot of whirring and clicking, and then "Hello? Mrs. Clarke?"

"Yes, Inspector Rand? Hi, the gypsies are on the move. They're no longer on the field behind Brush Row. My daughter is following them and suspects they're heading for Manchester. Apparently, there's a place there for travelers? Close to the city center?"

"Yes, it's on Dantzic Street. It was an official site, but it's closed, I'm afraid. That's not to say they won't go there, though. Okay, Mrs. Clarke. We'll head that way. Any change in course, please ring me."

"Have you a warrant?"

"Yes, we're all prepared. Oh, by the way, if you arrive before us, please don't approach anybody until we get there. Okay?"

"Yes, of course, Inspector." Clicking off my phone, I turned to Andy. "They've got the warrant sorted already."

"Good," replied Andy, "It seems they were taking us seriously after all."

"Yes, thank goodness."

The radio was on, and I could make out Vernon Kaye's voice chatting in his usual friendly way and then the traffic news, a woman with a nasally voice telling everybody to try not to drive today, to stay at home if at all possible, as the snow is causing havoc on the roads with miles of traffic at a standstill and little chance of a let-up within the next few hours.

She's right, I thought, as the snow was coming

down faster now, the car's wipers struggling to keep a clear windscreen so Andy had to hunch forward to see properly. I noticed his hands gripped the wheel, his knuckles white, and no doubt his heart racing just as mine was. There was a short silence before Andy said, "Jenny, you don't really think the death of Albie's wife and son excuses him somehow for what he might have done, do you?"

"Well, yes, I think the deaths will have affected him, but excuse him? No."

"Good," He shrugged, "I took it the wrong way then."

"Yes, I'm sorry," I took a deep breath, "That's not what I meant. Not at all." I shook my head, saying, "All I mean is that he might use it to get a lighter sentence."

"Oh, I see, yes you could be right," Reaching out a hand, he caressed my thigh and gave me a rueful grin when my phone beeped. A text message from Emma, *"I can see you in my mirror. I've pulled into a layby so we can stay together."*

Emma's little red car came into view, and as the traffic had slowed considerably, she slotted in easily in front of us, giving a flash of her lights for good measure. The traffic was crawling now, the snow coming down thicker and faster.

"They couldn't have picked a worse day to be

on the move," said Andy, "Are you bothered about the radio being on?" I shook my head as Andy switched it off, the only sound now being the swish-swish of the wipers across the windscreen. Up ahead, there was a never-ending stream of wagons and cars and caravans, crawling along at a snail's pace. Andy put what I was thinking into words.

"Actually," he said, "This weather is a God's send, really. It's slowed everything down and probably made Albie think twice about traveling further than Manchester."

"Yes, you're right," I replied, and then heartfelt, my hands clasped to my breasts, "Thank you, snow."

Andy laughed, throwing his head back, the wrinkles around his eyes appearing as if by magic, "You are funny, Jenny."

We crawled along, an inch at a time, slowly eating up the miles to our destination, keeping the caravans in sight. My heart thumped hard as I thought about what might happen when we arrived at Dantzic Street. After a couple of miles, the snow eased off, just white flakes floating in the air like fairies, and the traffic started to pick up speed, Emma still keeping just ahead of us.

"Oh, Andy, I can't wait. I just want to be there."

"Me too," He replied as he put his foot harder on the accelerator to keep up with the now-moving flow of traffic. White clouds suddenly fled away, and patches of blue sky appeared. Emma indicated to come off the A58, following the signs for Manchester town center. We drove along back street after back street, the car twisting and turning, until we saw a brown sign indicating the traveler's camp even though it was now closed. Emma indicated to pull over so, following suit, we pulled up behind her.

"Maybe Emma thinks we should walk now. It's possible somebody could see us if we go closer, and then they'd take off again."

"Yes, good idea," He gazed from the window, "I wonder if the police are here yet?"

Exchanging a worried glance, we got out of the car just as Emma got out of hers, carefully carrying baby Milly and then going to the boot for the pushchair. I smiled at her and, giving her a wave, shouted, "Emma," whilst Andy fumbled for my hand, gripping it hard as, taking deep breaths, we hurried towards her.

CHAPTER FIFTEEN

Present Day – January - Hidden Desires

My hand shaking, I gripped my phone as it purred like a cat, ringing over and over again. Was nobody going to answer? My heart beat like a drum. And then, at last, "Hello?"

"Jeanette?"

"Yes, Jeanette speaking. Who is this?"

Alarmed that she hadn't recognized my voice, or was she just kidding, I said, "It's me, Josh."

"What do you want?" The tone of her voice knocked my confidence right out of the window. I hadn't expected that, her voice laden with contempt. I stammered then, stumbling over my words. The words I thought I'd be able to say confidentially, pretty much my old self, my ego huge, "Oh, you're so full of yourself," as she always used to say.

"I miss you…I…"

It was her turn to be confident now as she said nastily, "Too bad! It's too late for that, Josh. You made your choice. Now leave me alone, don't call again."

She hung up. Yeah, Jeanette, the last person I'd expect to do that, but yeah, she hung up on me. I sat there then, glowering at my phone, the screen blank, an awful, terrifying blank. I half hoped for an apologetic text message, or a missed call, a voicemail dripping with sobs, but there was nothing, zilch.

My heart sank right down into my boots. If I'd been wearing boots, that is, but my feet were bare, my heart bare, my life bare. What should I do? My heart rose as I thought of Henry. I saw his face, his smile, his light blue eyes, and the sexy stubble that covered his cheeks and his chin. Pressing his number, I let it ring and ring, hoping he'd pick up, longing to hear his voice.

"Oh God," I thought, "Who is Josh going to end up with?" The ending of this story was still very much out there somewhere, swirling around in the ether but, unfortunately, just not in my own mind as yet. My publisher was getting impatient now. Urging me to finish the story, to get it done. My writing seemed to be taking a back seat yet again, especially now after all that had happened. Ah, life was so unexpected. You just never knew what was around the corner, did you?

I was at home, in my cozy caravan, the wood burner blaring out a beautiful heat, the flames mesmerizing to watch, cavorting sinuously, bright orange and red, behind the glass. Christmas and the New Year had come and gone, and all was back to normal. Although was it? For some people, maybe, but not for us, especially Andy. Hmm, was that a hint at what I'm going to tell you, dear reader?

I know, I know, I've left you holding on for dear life yet again, haven't I? A real cliffhanger at the end of the last chapter. "Yes," I heard you cry, "What happened? Did all the caravans head straight for the closed campsite on Dantzic Street? Did the police arrive, battling their way through the snow to save the day? What's the biggest question, though? The most important? Yes, I know exactly what you're thinking! Was Andy reunited with Susie?"

Okay, we'll go back to that snowy day. The snow that brought the traffic to a standstill, the snow that just kept falling until it was inches deep and in great drifts like a giant ice cream laying over fences and walls, a watery sunlight glinting a myriad of colors on unblemished fields and trees, their silvery white branches pointing up to the Heavens. We'd left our cars within walking distance of Dantzic Street. Do you remember? Here we go then. This was what happened.

"Mum, Andy," said Emma, giving us a nod, a bright smile creasing her face, "Here, hold Milly while I get the pushchair from the boot." Frosty air puffed from her mouth as she spoke.

I snuggled Milly into my body, Andy peering over my shoulder. She was wrapped up tight in a pink fluffy blanket, her tiny face peering out like a slice of cream cheese, and when she caught sight of us, her face creased into a smile, a real gummy smile. "She smiled at us," I said as I handed her over, and Emma tucked her into the pushchair, "A real proper smile."

"Oh, it'll be wind, Mum," she said, "She's done that before, and it's always wind."

"Oh well, you really have burst my bubble," I replied.

She giggled as we walked along, slipping and sliding on the slushy paths, Andy holding my hand so tightly. It was starting to ache, but I didn't say anything. I didn't want him to let go.

"It's possible," Andy said, "I remember Susie smiling at Fran and me when she was only a few months old."

Turning to him, I said, "Andy, I've just thought. Shouldn't you tell Fran about this?"

He shook his head, "Not yet. Let's just wait and see what happens. I don't want to get her hopes up." I nodded with understanding. If nothing came of this, the disappointment would be immense.

We neared Dantzic Street, and a caravan sped past, towed by an old green car that rattled and rolled, as it made its way along the street and drove through a pair of wide-open gates that looked as if they'd seen better days, in fact, the whole place looked run down and neglected, left to rot since its closure. Caravans and cars dotted the field, all of them covered in snow, little frozen squares like ice cubes in a freezer, and plenty of activity ensued as people got out of their cars, rubbing their hands and stamping their feet, shoulders hunched to their ears.

Boots crunched through the snow as they went to their caravans, lugging in bags of coal and wood kindling, thinking that a fire would be just the thing on a day like this. I noticed the old, dilapidated caravan that was Albie Shelby's, parked up with his wagon, the back still full of old scrap metal, and nudged Andy. He nodded, and I whispered to him, "So close and yet so far. The Inspector said not to approach anybody until they arrive."

He nodded, "Yes, he's right, but, oh boy, do I want to go over there and knock on his door."

I gave a rueful smile and said, "Me too," as my eyes roamed the field for a green well put together caravan (as Ruth Shelby had called it), the caravan owned by Susie, or should I say June, as she was now known, and her family of a husband and two little boys. The snow had stopped now, petered out at last, and the sky was blue, all the white clouds gone, melted away by the tepid sun. Birds fluttered around the trees, dislodging the snow that coated their branches and speckling the ground like icing sugar.

At last, the police were here, pulling up with a screech at the curb in an unmarked car. The Detective Inspector leaned from his open window, "We think the best bet is that we stay here and watch while you two go in. We'll be here if anything untoward happens."

"What about my daughter and the baby?" I asked, noticing Emma's pinched face and red nose, "It's so cold out here."

"She can get in the car with us." He turned to the Sergeant, "Ben, if you wouldn't mind giving the young lady some help with the pushchair." Sergeant Lofthouse sprang from the car and approached Emma, who, with a small smile of thanks, got into the back of the car, baby Milly in her arms as the Sergeant folded the pushchair and put it into the boot, closing it with a click.

A shiny black car towing a green caravan passed us as Andy and I walked through the gates. I noticed a young couple inside, two children sitting in the back. I stopped and stood, one hand over my mouth. I could barely breathe as Andy, noticing I wasn't beside him, came to an abrupt halt and said, "Jenny? What's wrong?" and when I didn't reply, "Jenny?"

My hand shaking, I pointed forward, swallowing hard as if something had somehow become lodged in my throat. Butterflies fluttered in my stomach, "Look." I swallowed again. My throat was dry, parched as if I needed water, gallons of it, "Look, Andy, "I pointed to the green caravan, "Maybe we won't need to speak to Mr. Shelby after all."

Slowly, we walked forward, our boots crunching on the path, watching the black car towing the green caravan as it maneuvered expertly into a parking space. The passenger door opened, and a woman got out. She was bundled up for the cold, wearing black leggings and a thick puffa-type jacket, a bright scarf around her neck, gloves on her hands, and sturdy walking boots on her feet. She wore a woolly hat that hid her hair, yet some had escaped, framing her face with tendrils of silky ash blonde.

The driver, a tall, slim man with a shock of black hair, joined her, and the children clambered out of the back seat, excited to be in the snow, calling in high-pitched voices for mummy and daddy, to watch me, watch me, reminding me suddenly of that sweet four-year-old girl from so long ago. A smile lit up her face, and her green eyes flashed in a sudden shaft of sunlight. "Be careful, you two," she said, "Bobby, look after your little brother."

We were closer now, a trail of deep footprints behind us as we walked further and further forward. Birds twittered in the trees, and in the distance, rushing traffic could be heard, the beeping of horns and closer, the gentle murmur of voices, the thunk of car doors, and then music and garbled voices as radios and televisions were switched on. Already, the sun was sinking, a spreading bright orange glow on the horizon, indicating that within just a few hours, this little part of the world would be in darkness.

She looked up and saw us, her smile suddenly replaced by a frown. Shaking her head slightly, she walked forward, her boots crunching on the snow, a hand to her brow shielding her eyes from the bright orange glare, before stopping and simply standing, her eyes wide, both hands to her mouth, "Daddy?"

Andy smiled and, slowly, as if unsure what to do, held out his arms, "Susie?"

She flew towards him, her arms open wide, "Oh, Daddy."

Quickly, I pulled my phone from my pocket, and with one click, I captured the moment.

***

"Hi, just me, Dave, checking in. Happy New Year! Not long, and I'll be in your neck of the woods. I can't wait to see your cozy boat and the life you've made for yourself since I've been gone. A life on the ocean waves, eh? Lol. Look out for me. That romantic time of the year isn't that far away, is it Jenny? You know what I mean, don't you? Mr. Valentine is going to call!"

***

All three men sat at a square wooden table, the two

police officers facing Mr. Shelby. A jug of water and glasses sat in the middle of the table. Andy and I had been allowed to watch the proceedings upstairs through a two-way window. The interview was being recorded, and Sergeant Ben Lofthouse pressed the button on the recording device, and Detective Inspector Jack Rand began to speak.

Police Interview with Mr. Albert Gordon Shelby, Todmorden Police Station Present – Detective Inspector Jack Rand, Sergeant Ben Lofthouse, and Mr. Albert Gordon Shelby

Detective Inspector Jack Rand (DIJR) – Mr. Shelby, take your mind back to June nineteen ninety and the kidnap of four-year-old Susie Valentine. What can you tell us about that?

Mr. Albert Gordon Shelby (AGS) – A long silence.

(DIJR) – Mr. Shelby, I need you to cooperate with us. Please answer the question. You were seen outside the Toddy Tots Day Nursery sitting in a blue van, registration number 198 NCG. Did you have a van of this description?"

(AGS) – *(After much clearing of his throat).* Yeah, gave up the ghost years ago, did that van. A good, reliable motor for a long time, though. *(Another long silence)*

(DIJR) – We need you to cooperate with us, Mr. Shelby.

(AGS) - *Taking a deep breath.* I wanted a boy, really, because the baby that died was a boy. But she came out of the nursery first, and I panicked, thought I should take my chance before it was too late, before somebody saw me or recognized my van.

Sergeant Ben Lofthouse (SBF) - So, Mr. Shelby, you're admitting then that you did kidnap Susie Valentine in June nineteen ninety?

(AGS) - I wasn't thinking straight. I saw her. She came running out of the nursery, calling she was for somebody called Jenny. She was alone and, yes, I took her.

(DIJR) - When you took Susie Valentine, Mr. Shelby, did it never cross your mind that you were depriving her of a life with her own two parents? Two parents who loved her very much?

(AGS) - *(Adamantly shaking his head).* No, I never thought of them and, anyway, who's to say I didn't give her a better life. I brought her up well with her sister, Anita. I named her June cos it was June when I took her, and I've given her a good life. She's traveled all over the country. I've fed her, clothed her, and loved her for the past thirty-three years, and I consider her to be my own daughter.

(SBF) - Did you know, Mr. Shelby, that Susie's mother, Mrs. Francesca Louise Valentine, was pregnant when you took her daughter? And that due to the stress of Susie being taken from her, she subsequently lost her baby?

(AGS) – *(Swallowing hard, the snake tattoo moving sinuously on his neck).* No, I didn't know that, and, well, I gotta say, it's a shame.

(DIJR) – Even though you consider her as your own daughter, Mr. Shelby, did you hear the words Susie Valentine said when she saw, her biological father, Mr. Andrew Colin Valentine, after having no contact with him for thirty-three years?

(AGS) – *(Swallowing harder)* No, I didn't hear what she said.

(SBF) – She called him Daddy, Mr. Shelby. Do you hear that, Mr. Shelby? Susie Valentine, also known as June Shelby, called Mr. Andrew Colin Valentine, Daddy.

To the intense shock and surprise of the two Police Officers and myself and Andy watching, Mr. Shelby began to cry. Great heaving sobs, his shoulders moving up and down. Fat tears rolled down his cheeks, highlighting the black tattooed cross, and the tattoo around his neck moved sinuously as if it were a real living and breathing snake.

(AGS) – I'd lost my wife and son only months before that. I was desperate, unhinged, maybe. It was like a dream. One minute, I was watching this lovely little girl, and the next, I had her in my van, strapped into the seat next to me. I didn't hurt her; I loved her from the start, and I've cared for her.

(SBF) – She remembered her Daddy, Mr. Shelby. After thirty-three years, she still remembered her biological father, despite the fact she was only four when she was taken.

(AGS) – *A long silence.*

(SBF) – Was Susie Valentine upset, Mr. Shelby, when you took her? Did she cry or protest in any way?"

(AGS) – *Adamantly.* No!

(DIJR) – Are you sure about that, Mr. Shelby?

(AGS) – *A long silence.*

(DIJR) – Are you aware, Mr. Shelby, that even after all this time, there are still grave consequences for the kidnap of a child, and when this case goes to court, there could well be a prison sentence?"

(AGS) – I wasn't in my right mind, though, was I? I'd only just suffered a bereavement. *(There was a sly, calculating look on his face).* Maybe the consequences will be lighter, community service or summat like that?

(DIJR) – I wouldn't count on that, Mr. Shelby. I really wouldn't.

(SBF)– Just one other thing, Mr. Shelby. We've been told that June had dark hair as a child, but it's blonde now. Did her hair color change as she grew up, or did you conceal it?

(AGS) – *(A slight hesitation).* Yeah, alright, I've told you everything else. It was a wig.

(SBF) – You put the wig on her after you took her?

(AGS) – Yes.

(DIJR) — Have you anything to tell us about that day?

A long, painful silence ensued before Detective Inspector Jack Rand declared the interview over and turned off the recording device. Andy and I watched as Mr. Shelby was led from the room, the door swinging shut behind them, and the interview room left empty, the jug of water untouched, the chairs askew.

"I hope he gets life," commented Andy, "But I doubt he will."

"No, he'll play the depression card," I replied, "As I thought he would."

"Yes," Andy looked at me, his eyes narrowed, "You said something about that before, and you're right. I could tell by his face that that's exactly what he's planning to do," He turned towards me, "You were right about the wig."

I nodded, "Yes," And then, "How has Fran taken all this?"

"I don't know," Andy replied, "She's made a new life." I squeezed his arm in sympathy, "It's too hurtful for her."

We walked to the door, "Shall we go home?"

"Yes, although maybe we could call and see

Susie first if you want to?"

I smiled, "Yes, let's go and see your daughter."

"And my grandchildren," He replied proudly, "And my son-in-law."

"Yes, all of them," I agreed, thinking suddenly of my parents and my sister, Maisie, all gone now, yet I had Emma and Jack, and baby Milly, precious memories of my husband, Frank, even some good times with Dave, and another chance right now at family life with Andy. We left the room and walked out into a cold but sunny day, piles of dirty snow still laying on the ground like mini-icebergs. I shivered as I zipped up my coat and pulled on a pair of gloves, adjusted my scarf. Hand in hand, we walked down the steps and into the street.

"Do you know, though, Jenny, there's one thing they didn't mention in that interview."

"What?"

"That Susie recognized you, too. Straight away. It was amazing, really."

"Yes, I was very happy about that."

He nudged me in the ribs, "Show's how unforgettable you are."

"I wouldn't go that far, Andy."

"You wouldn't? I would."

"You're daft."

"Jenny," He pulled me to a standstill, "I've been

wanting to say this for a long time," His green eyes gazed into mine, "I love you."

My heart rose as I said the very same words back, "I love you, too."

He nodded, "Well, that's okay then."

He gave me a sexy wink and took my hand as we walked quickly, urgently to go and see Susie.

CHAPTER SIXTEEN

Present Day – 14th February - "Hidden Desires"

"I'd made up my mind. I really had. I was alone, but I didn't know for how long, so now was the time." Rushing upstairs, I went into the bedroom, pulled a suitcase down from the top of the wardrobe, and flung it on the bed. I searched through my clothes, pulling out jeans, trousers, shirts, tee shirts, and piled it all into the suitcase. I squashed in shoes, trainers, underwear, and toiletries and then, pressing the lid down hard, zipped it up.

I lugged the suitcase downstairs and left it in the hallway whilst I grabbed a piece of paper and a pen. Sitting at the kitchen table, I wrote this, "Dear Henry, I'm sorry, but I'm going. This isn't a spur of the moment decision but something that's been brewing in my head for a while. You know as well as I do that our relationship isn't working. I care for you, I do, and I wish we still had something going, but it's impossible. I think I've got all my stuff, although it's too bad really if I haven't, because I won't be coming back.

All my love always, Josh."

I shrugged on my coat and, taking a trilby hat from the coat stand, carefully put it on my head. I picked up my suitcase and walked to the door, making sure I left the key in the little china pot on the old Victorian dresser, something we'd bought so carefully together only a few weeks before. I left then, closing the door firmly behind me, hurrying down the steps and into the street, my heart growing lighter and lighter with every single step I took.

"There," I thought, "The end," I took a deep breath, "It was the only way. Josh had to leave. I couldn't choose between his future with Jeanette or Henry, so I picked neither of them. Good move, eh? One that I'm sure my publisher would be glad of when she received the manuscript."

I stood up and stretched luxuriously, arching my back like a cat. Just like Sydney who slept soundly beside me, her tiny body moving up and down like bellows. My phone buzzed with a text message from Andy, *"Hi Jenny, Happy Valentine's Day. See you in the pub about 12.30pm? Vanessa and her husband are coming now as well as all the family. I can't wait to see you x."*

My heart rose at the thought of our planned Valentine's meal in a pub in Hebden Bridge. Apparently, *"The White Lion"* did excellent meals at fairly reasonable prices, so we'd booked in for all eleven of us. I couldn't wait to see Emma, Jack and baby Milly, Susie and her husband, Bob, and the two boys, Bobby and Vince and now Vanessa and her husband, George? Was he called George? Hmm, I'd need to check that one.

Glancing at my watch, I saw I had only an hour to go so, panicking now, wondering what I should wear, I clicked off my laptop, so glad I'd finished the book at last. I felt lighter somehow and a sense of accomplishment flooded through me as I jumped in the shower and then wandered into the bedroom to search through my clothes, undecided between a dress or smart jeans. I chose the dress, quickly slipped it over my head, and then put on thick tights and knee-high boots.

Gazing in the mirror whilst putting on dangly earrings, mascara, and a slick of lipstick, I thought of Albie Shelby and the up-and-coming court case, hoping fervently that justice would be served after what he'd done. How he'd pulled a small but tight-knit family apart and caused years of grieving, so much so that even now, Fran, Andy's ex-wife, was too upset to see Susie. Oh, how I hoped she'd change her mind soon. I knew that Andy wanted her to reconsider and that Susie would love to see her, but she understood and was prepared to wait. What a lovely young woman she'd turned out to be.

A loud rap on the door brought me out of my reverie, making me jump. Excitedly, I flung it open, hoping it was Andy, as a valentine surprise, to be met with the sight of the largest bouquet of red roses I'd ever seen. I gazed at them nestled within their shiny leaves, interspersed with delicate strands of baby's breath, emitting a sweet, intoxicating odor that hovered in the air. I looked at the gloved hands that held them and then further down to the feet encased in a pair of shiny black shoes until a face I hadn't seen for a long time peered around the edge of the crackly transparent wrapper, "I told you to look out for me today, didn't I Jenny? Mr. Valentine calling."

My heart thumped hard, and, no doubt, my eyes were on stalks as I put my hands to my mouth and said, "Oh my God, Dave."

"The very man," he said, pushing the flowers towards me, "Well, aren't you going to invite me in?"

Taking the massive bouquet from him, I reluctantly opened the door a little wider, and he slipped inside, his eyes darting everywhere, taking in the interior of my little boat. He looked about the same, a little fatter perhaps, but he was quite well dressed in a pair of jeans and a blue shirt, a thick jacket over the top, "Wow, I can't believe this." He stood there shaking his head, "This place seems so tiny after my flat in New York. You should see it, Jenny, you'd be impressed."

"No doubt I would," I said as I went to the kitchen and put the flowers in the sink, "Thank you for the flowers. Would you like a coffee?"

"No thanks, I'm taking you out for a drink, Madam, and a meal if you like. How about that?"

"Oh, I'm sorry, Dave, but I've made plans, I'm afraid," I motioned with my hand as I sat down on the settee, "But sit down, we can have a chat before I go," I looked at my watch, "I've got about fifteen minutes yet. You really should have texted me to let me know you were coming."

"I only arrived here last night," He gave me an assessing look from the top of my head to the tip of my toes, "Oh yeah, I wondered why you were all dressed up. Who you got plans with, Jenny?"

"My boyfriend, Andy, and some other people."

He stood there in front of me, his legs spread wide, hands on his hips, "Oh, your boyfriend, Andy, eh? Well, well, I told you ages ago, I was going to call on Valentine's Day."

"Oh, Dave, it's not just about that. We're meeting up with people we haven't seen for ages. A nice meal out that just happens to be on Valentine's Day."

"Yeah, right, you soon replaced me, didn't you, Jenny? I don't think you ever missed me one bit.

"Oh, I did, Dave, for a long time until I realized we wanted different things. You love New York, and I love being here," I opened my arms wide, "In Hebden Bridge. It's beautiful here, look," We gazed out of the window at the canal, the water rippling, a fine mist hovering above, and birds swimming gracefully, speckling the brown water with vibrant colors of green, white, and black.

He moved closer to the settee and stood over me, the great bulk of him menacing, making my heart beat hard and fast. I swallowed, my throat dry as a bone. I really wished Dave would go and that Andy would come. If only I'd arranged to meet him here. Secretly, I glanced at my watch. The time was getting on. I should be leaving now.

"Cancel your plans and come out with me," he growled, "It's the least you can do, Jenny."

I stood up, my legs shaking, and reached for my coat, saying calmly, "No, Dave, I can't. People are expecting me. They'll wonder where I am if I don't turn up." Buttoning up my coat, I picked up my phone and placed it in my bag, putting the strap of the bag over my head and across my body."

Suddenly, he lunged forward, pushing me against the wall and pinning my arms at my side. I was taken aback, winded, the back of my head on fire where it had thumped into the wall. Tears sprang into my eyes, "Dave, what are you doing? Have you gone mad?"

"Just do as I say, Jenny, and cancel those silly plans of yours."

"No, I won't. Don't you realize how stupid you're being? I could call the police on you and that isn't a good look for Dave Ledgard, big shot IT man with a grand apartment and epic job in New York, is it?"

He gripped me harder and glared at me, his face very close to mine, his eyes tiny pinpricks of what looked like hatred. "You've changed, Jenny, you've really changed."

A hot rage shot through me, and before I knew what I was doing, all the pent-up stress of the past few months came pouring out, "Oh, Dave, you're so full of yourself now. It's all about you, isn't it? Don't you realize how well off you are in your life? You've never had a child stolen away from you, have you? And spent your life searching and searching, not knowing if that child is dead or alive?"

"What are you talking about? You're rambling, Jenny."

"Andy's daughter was taken when she was only four years old, and it's only recently he's been reunited with her. She's thirty-seven now, Dave. Thirty-seven! He endured thirty-three years without her, but he didn't give up. He just kept on searching, and now, today, we're having a long-awaited meal with her and her husband and children. Those are the plans I have that you want me to cancel, Dave." Tired now, my throat sore from talking and stress, I sagged against the wall, uncaring now at what he might do next.

Dave moved away slightly, letting go of my arms, just as my phone lit up and started to ring, buzzing away in my bag. Slowly, I sank to the floor, legs outstretched in front of me, tears streaming down my face, and yes, dear reader, tears that were ruining the make-up I'd applied so carefully. I was aware of Dave still standing, towering over me, yet his voice was strained as he said, "So what. Why should I care about what happened to your new boyfriend?"

"To make you think of other people's lives and not just your own. You didn't have a clue what's been happening in my life. And I doubt you cared. Now go, Dave, go back to New York. Have a good life. Otherwise, I'll have no choice but to call the police."

I didn't look up but my hopes rose as I saw his shiny black shoes walking towards the door, but then plummeted again as they stopped and he turned around. I tensed, waiting for him to grab me again, for one final act of what seemed pent-up anger, but all he said was, "I know you don't believe in the hype, but you can keep the flowers," and then the shoes disappeared, and the door banged shut.

I heaved a massive sigh of relief and tried to stand up, but I was shaking so hard I kept falling again and sliding down the wall. Retrieving my phone from my bag, I glanced at the screen, which showed a missed call from Andy and then there was a tap at the door.

"Who is it?" I asked, afraid for a split second that Dave had changed his mind and come back to terrorize me, and yet, would he knock if that was his intention?

"Jenny, it's me," and, to my relief, Andy was there, his eyes widening as he saw me sitting on the floor with my back to the wall. "Good God, what's happened? Who was that fella I just saw walking away with a face like thunder?" He hunkered down next to me looking as gorgeous as ever in jeans, a white shirt, his long black overcoat over the top, his face with his stubbly beard handsome and rugged.

"That was my ex, Dave," I said tearfully, sobs rising into my throat, "Oh, Andy, I was so afraid."

Holding out a hand, Andy helped me to stand up and then pulled me close, rubbing my back with the palm of his hand, "Hey, it's okay. He didn't hurt you, did he?"

I shook my head, and Andy said, "If he ever comes near you again, Jenny..." He let his words hang in the air as he gazed at me, his eyes dark green pools.

"He won't. I threatened him with the police. And, anyway, he'll be going back to New York soon."

"But what's his problem? Didn't *he* leave *you*?"

"Yes, but when he saw I was okay with him

going, happy even without him, he wanted me back."

"I was so worried about you. I knew something was wrong when you didn't turn up at the pub. You're never late."

Tearfully, I said, "I couldn't get away."

Putting his arms around my shoulders, he said, "Don't cry. You look so beautiful, and your dress is lovely."

"How can you say that? I look awful. My make-up's all ruined now. I'll have to patch it up. It won't take long."

Shaking his head and smiling, Andy said, "You always look beautiful to me, but go ahead," He waved a hand, "And re-do your face, I'll wait. We've plenty of time."

Rushing into the bathroom, I said, "Aren't we already late?"

"No, um, actually, I wanted time alone with you beforehand, so I told everybody else to meet at 1.30pm."

"Time alone?" I shouted from the bathroom.

"Yes, there's something I want to ask you."

Curiously, I peered around the bathroom door, "Oh yeah, what's that?"

He grinned, "Wait and see," and then airily, his nose in the air, "All good things come to those who wait."

"I told Dave about you," I said as we walked hand in hand along the towpath into Hebden Bridge, "About you being reunited with Susie. I didn't mean to, but it all just came out." It was a fine afternoon, the sun shining and sparkling on the water. There were a lot of people about, walkers as well as cyclists and runners, while swans padded gracefully and naughty geese hissed.

He looked at me with a frown, "Why?"

"So, he could put things into perspective," I said and then shrugged, "So everything's not all about him. He should appreciate what he's got, a great job and life in New York, which is exactly what he wanted when he left me."

"Yeah, I see, so it would jolt him into manning up, stopping his sniveling, and leaving you alone?"

I nodded and smiled, "Yes, something like that."

"Well, it worked, didn't it?"

I laughed, "Yes, I think it did in the end."

"Here." He indicated with a sideways nod of his head, "Come and sit down for a minute."

"We'll be late, Andy," I said, worried, yet sitting down next to him, wondering what he was going to say.

"Jenny, do you realize that without you, I wouldn't have Susie back?"

"That's not true, Andy, I..."

"Ssh," he pressed a finger to my lips, "I'd been searching for her for years. No matter what you say, you helped me get her back."

"Okay, we worked together."

He smiled at me and then, fumbling in his pocket, pulled out a small black box, "Jenny," He took a deep breath, "I really can't imagine my life without you now. Will you marry me?"

"Andy, I, oh…"

"It doesn't have to be straight away," he said hurriedly, "We can have a long engagement."

My heart beating like a drum, I stammered again, "Oh, Andy, I…oh…"

"Does that mean yes?"

"Yes! Yes, I mean, yes. Yes! But, aren't we too old for a long engagement?"

Laughing, he threw his head back, showing off that lovely slice of hairy chest at the open neck of his shirt.

A couple of elderly ladies eyed us as they walked slowly by, smiling and nudging each other, watching as Andy opened the box and carefully retrieved a silver ring set with a beautiful emerald stone and, gently taking my hand, slipped it on my finger, "I hope you like it; the emerald matches your eyes."

"It's beautiful, oh Andy, it's beautiful…"

"Hey, don't cry," He shook his head, "There's

no way you're repairing your make-up now, or we really will be late."

Laughing and crying, I flung my arms around his neck and whispered, "Andy, I love you."

"I love you, too."

There was a flutter of applause from the two ladies, one of them saying, "Good for you, love, I'd marry him if he asked me to…"

"Handsome, isn't he?" agreed the other.

"Come on," said Andy, his smile creating those dimples, one in each cheek, "Let's go meet with our families."

We walked on then into the town, our hands entwined, happy to be together. Just the two of us, me and the lovely Andy, my very own sweet valentine.

THE END

Debbie Chase (married name Debbie Spink) was born in Emsworth in Hampshire, in 1959 but has lived in West Yorkshire since 1979. She is the eldest of five children (two sisters and two brothers) and has many nieces and nephews, great-nieces and nephews, aunties, uncles and cousins, having come from a very large family. She has been married since 1984 and has one daughter, Lara, and three cats, Ruby, Teddy, and Maurice.

She has always been a reader and has enjoyed writing since school. Her proudest moment being when she achieved an A+ for an essay! She has had many short stories and poems for adults and children published in books and magazines. She has written five self-published books, the first being part fact/part fiction and called "You to Me Are Everything." The second book based on a real-life pet-sitting job is called "The Confessions of a Pet Sitter (from the Pet's Point of View), and the third, the sequel to that book, "What a Catastrophe (Teddy's Tale). The fourth book is a book of poems, "I Wasn't There," and the fifth is a murder mystery, "Whatever Happened to George England."

She has also had nine pocket novels published with "My Weekly" magazine, "Planning on Love," "Romance on the Run," "Puppy Love,," "Esther Baby," "Double Trouble" also known as "The Doppelganger," "The Crying Game," "Rachel's War," "Birdie" and "Number One Fan." Her other novels, "Educating Maggie" "A Step Back in Time," "Ruby Tuesday," "The Haunting of Pear Tree Cottage," "The Gift," and the "Mannequin Mystery," are published here with World Castle Publishing, with another novel "My Sweet Valentine," coming soon. All her novels are available to buy online.

Her hobbies are weight training, walking, running, yoga, kettlebell workouts and Pilates. After many years of office work, pub work, and shop work, she is now partially retired and, as well as writing books, works part-time as a Dog Walker/Pet Sitter (Woof Woof Walkies) with her daughter and as an Examination Invigilator in a local school, and is also a House Experience Volunteer at East Riddlesden Hall, an old manor house open to the public, in Keighley.

Printed in Dunstable, United Kingdom

77913700R00139